On Track

A Diana Jeffries Mystery

Barbara Pearson-Rac

DEDICATION

To my mother Phyllis. She never laughed or raised her eyebrow when I told her I wanted to write a novel! Her belief in me was my inspiration.

CONTENTS

ACKNOWLEDGMENTS

Writing this book has been an exciting journey. So many people gave their support and insights; I just hope I left no one out. But, the inspiration came from the folks on the train, Stuart Ornstein, Laurie Price, and Marion Sykes who were the basis for the gang. And of course, our conductor, who spread the word that he was a featured character in the book, which created quite a buzz among the other Metro-North conductors. And then there were my fellow commuters, who always added their "two cents." But that was the fun part: While standing on the train platform, we noodled the name of the book, while I proofed pages on the train ride into the city as peering eyes critiqued the text. I still have fellow commuters asking me, "What's happening with the book?"

I reached out to professional writers for their feedback. My late Uncle Herbert gave me an added perspective; Elizabeth Hilts gave me great advice on plot structure, and Matthew Roshkow helped me understand the need to work on the voice of my characters.

But my real inspiration came from those that were just readers. As I was writing the book, I shared my chapters with Raquel Retta, who pressed me for the next chapter because she was hooked on how the story was unfolding. My son-in-law, Steve Rochette, delved with great energy into reading, supporting, and encouraging my efforts. Fred Bloxham and Karen Schiffres spent a weekend reading the pages, and their enthusiasm gave me the confidence to finish. My husband, Frank, sat in the dining room with pen in hand, editing and enjoying the read. My daughter, Sara, the real writer in the family, helped me tweak my words and has always been there, giving me a nudge to publish. And my sister, Carol Schaeffer made many thoughtful and terrific suggestions that were very much appreciated.

Susan Santangelo, now on her fifth book, began her writing career when I started this book and has since become a very successful author. She has truly been my role model—we're two seniors switching gears—and I hope I can keep up with her.

Sara Brzowsky, my editor, gave me new insights on sentence structure, but her greatest contribution was her enthusiasm for the book which convinced me I had truly become an author.

And thanks to Miggs Burroughs, who brought my cover concept to life!

CHAPTER 1

JUST ANOTHER DAY

Diana sat at her kitchen table, coffee mug in one hand and her latest mystery read in the other. She opened the book and began to pick up where she left off:

Detective Jonah Miles, looking more haggard than usual, with deep creases and dark circles underneath his penetrating blue eyes, his hair in disarray and his clothes with more wrinkles than his aging face, paced back and forth while the suspects sat staring at him, mesmerized by the story that was unfolding.

"Wednesday evening, as you recall, was a night that kept the most adventurous from leaving their homes. The moon was negligible, the stars were hidden and the fog was dense and foreboding creating a dangerous atmosphere. No one in their right minds was out and about. It was an evening for homebodies, warm fires and good books. But Linda Pace left the safety of her home as she did every evening to walk Clarence, her faithful ten year old Labrador Retriever. After all, she wasn't going very far, just to the middle of her lawn. Clarence was never leashed because he stayed on their three acre property. We're told that Linda would nudge her elderly pet by strolling onto the lawn until he would run off to do his business. This evening, Linda had already prepared for bed. She was wearing a flimsy nightgown covered by her raincoat. She stood quietly waiting for Clarence

to return. Unknown to her, someone was lurking in the nearby bushes, timing their attack. When Clarence was safely away from his owner, the attacker quietly approached Linda, gun in hand and shot her once in the back of the head. Linda fell forward, dying instantly. Clarence discovered her body and sat by her side howling until morning when the gardener discovered them." The detective stopped, and glanced from one person to another, staring into their frightened eyes, "Everyone in this room had a motive to murder Linda Pace, and I'm here today to expose you, arrest you, and supply irrefutable evidence to put you away for life. So, let's start with you, Mr. Arogon..."

* * *

"Diana, Diana, Earth to Diana!" Josh yelled.

"What, what is it?" Diana asked, annoyed.

"Hurry, you're going to be late for the train, close the book," Josh urged.

"You know it's Metro Monday, and we exchange books on the train," Diana responded as she took another gulp of coffee. "I haven't finished mine yet. I only have a few pages left and Detective Miles is about to expose the killer. I have no idea who did it. This one's a real nail-biter."

"Read it on the train before you swap! You know how you like to get to the platform early to get 'the spot,'" Josh teased.

"You jest, but the spot is vital to our survival. The door opens just where I stand so I can grab the four seats I need for my gang," Diana said.

"Yeah, right, let's get going before someone else usurps your spot," Josh said, winking as he gently pushed his wife toward the garage door and the car.

As they entered the garage, Josh hit the button on the wall, activating the garage door and revealing a picture-perfect New England winter scene. It was a panorama of glistening white: icicles hanging from the eaves, snow-covered tree limbs, and a cap of white blanketing the rugged stone wall. It was a magnificent scene—except to Diana and Josh, two New England pragmatists about to commute to work. What *they* saw was that the wind was howling, the snow was three-feet deep, the temperature was zero, and the wind chill minus-twenty degrees. It was a raw, windy, cold morning.

Diana sighed. "I can't remember the last time I was ever warm outside," she said. "But this is the life we chose when we decided to live in the town of Westport, Connecticut."

Westport was an idyllic New England coastal community about fifty miles north of Manhattan. It maintained the aura of a small town, yet its residents were very cosmopolitan, in part because of their proximity to New York City. Many of those who worked in the City didn't spend enough quality time in town, but Diana had met some wonderful neighbors aboard the Metro-North commuter train, and they had become an interesting extension of her community and best of all, great friends.

* * *

Diana arrived on the platform with plenty of time to grab "the spot." To avoid freezing, she wore a white wool hat pulled down near her glasses, a green scarf wrapped around her neck and face, and her very warm coyote fur coat and brown shearling-lined leather boots. She waited for her gang, pondering the advantages of a burka.

Diana Jeffries, a professor of sociology, known to some as "Doc," was a powerhouse. She was tall, thin, and regal-looking with flowing, chestnut, curly hair. The chestnut color came straight from a bottle. Diana was sixty years old, proud of it, and still gorgeous, wrinkles and all. She considered herself semi-retired. As a tenured professor, she had cut back on her teaching schedule at Hunter College and now concentrated on research at New York Medical School. Occasionally, she consulted with the New York City Police Department. Diana described herself as the "queen" of part-time jobs, but that hardly described her busy schedule. With a grown daughter and a husband who was a well-known and quite busy litigator, Diana felt she had time to pursue her own interests, of which there were many! Reading mysteries was one of her passions. When she met the gang—Allen, Margie, and Beverly—she discovered that they shared her passion. They decided to form the Metro-North Book Club and exchange books every two weeks.

Diana had been riding on the train with the gang for almost five years and they had formed a wonderful friendship.

"Diana, I'm freezing," Beverly gasped as she arrived on the platform, dressed in a fur-lined coat, hat, double gloves, and Ugg boots.

"You're running a bit late, catch your breath. You'll have a heart attack."

"I know, but my car was covered with a layer of ice this morning, and I couldn't open the door," Beverly said. "Ron had already left for work, so I had to work on the door myself." Beverly depended on her husband, Ron, for anything she considered major, and this definitely fell into that category.

"Oh, here comes Allen, the train must be seconds away. He times his arrival perfectly. Where's Margie?" Diana turned her head to look for her friend.

"I'm here, I'm here," Margie cried out, huffing. She was always running late.

In train years, Metro-North cars were thirty-five years old, translating into about eighty man years, so the ride into the City could not be considered comfortable or luxurious but rather a miracle! As the train limped into the station now, a crowd formed around Diana. All eyes were on the doors, anticipating where they would actually open. And, as on most days, they opened right on the "spot." Diana charged in and found their usual four seats—two seats facing another two seats. There was little if any legroom. Diana guessed that thirty-five years ago commuters must have been shorter! But the seating was cozy and gave the gang a chance to chat and catch up on new gossip before they pulled out their morning reading material.

The seating was always the same. Diana and Beverly rode backwards, sitting opposite Margie and Allen. The gang also had a morning train ritual. Once Beverly carefully removed her coat and placed it in the overhead rack, she sat down and handed Allen the *New York Times* sports page. Now their commute could officially begin.

"Is everybody settled?" Margie asked.

"No," Diana replied, "Give me five minutes to finish my book. I know, I know. It's Metro Monday, and I'm always the one to finish last, but I had papers to grade last night and didn't have time to read on the train home."

"Excuses, excuses," Beverly said. She was smiling. She knew how upset Diana got when she missed a deadline. "We'll give you five minutes before the switch."

Diana pulled out her book and began to read. Allen started reading the sports page, Beverly turned to the Op Eds, while Margie read a report on a new prescription drug plan. Margie was the Director of SOAP, Society of Aging Parents, a competitor of AARP. She spent a great deal of time lobbying in Washington and was on the leading edge of those defining the problems related to caring for the needs of the elderly.

Margie *looked* like a lobbyist and was perfect for the job. She was sixty-three years old with a beautiful face but enough wrinkles to be believable, had perfectly teased bleached-blond hair, donned tailored suits, was organized and renowned as a dynamic public speaker. But, when it came to taking risks, she was a bit conservative and cautious. That was a positive when working in politics. Legislators could take years to act, and Margie had a ton of patience.

What a perfect relationship!

Diana closed the book, "Let's do it!" She handed her book to Margie. Beverly reached into her commuter bag and handed the latest Elizabeth Peters mystery to Diana. Meanwhile, Allen handed his James Patterson to Beverly, while Margie handed Allen her Patricia Cornwall.

"Who's Reginald Thomas?" Margie asked, glancing down at the book Diana had given her.

"I have no idea," Diana said. "I was bookless, went into a bookstore and grabbed what looked like an interesting read. It's his first novel, and they're always fun. It was good! A nice tongue-in-cheek mystery with tons of suspects. It'll keep you guessing. I promise."

"I'll give it a try," Margie said. "Your book reviews are generally on the money.

"So, now that we've got the Metro Monday book exchange taken care of, any new tidbits?" Diana asked.

"I have a tid," Allen offered.

"A 'tid'?" Margie asked.

"Yes, I found another great airfare to Florida."

"You're going again?" Diana asked.

"In March. I have friends coming in today, and they just spent $300 one way to get here."

"That's a lot, I just got tickets for $160 round trip," Margie boasted.

"It costs $300 just to go to Cleveland," Allen continued.

Beverly pulled her head out of the paper. "Who wants to go the Cleveland?" she asked.

"No one," Margie said.

"Well," Allen responded, "that's not true. I have clients in

Cleveland and go there all the time."

"Enough about Cleveland," Beverly said. "I have a 'bit.' Margie, I cut this out of the paper. It's a replacement for Botox. Only $135 for six ounces." She rummaged through her commuter bag to retrieve the ad and handed it to Margie. Diana looked at her two friends, admiring their wonderful appearance. And yet, they were always on the lookout for ways to recover their youth. Aging was not something they accepted gracefully.

"Does it work?" Margie asked.

"I have no idea. I don't even know what's in it, but maybe we can share a jar and see."

Allen smirked as he listened to the girls gab about age-reducing products. Allen had just turned seventy three but didn't look a day over sixty five. He was five feet eight inches tall, thin, agile, and active with salt-and-pepper hair and a broad, endearing smile. He was the most predictable person Diana knew. She often teased him that 'routine' was his middle name. He ate at the same restaurants, visited the same stores, watched the same television shows and took the same vacations. In his own way, he was a bit of a flake. He could be forgetful—misplacing his wallet or leaving his morning cup of coffee perched on the roof of his car—but somehow and fortunately he never lost any of the diamonds that he sold.

Allen had many pluses, including his jewelry business. In addition, since he'd been commuting for fifty years, he was able to introduce Diana, Margie, and Beverly to many of the Metro-North conductors, including Tom, who had been their conductor for many years. Since the day he'd met him, Tom referred to the three as Al's Girls. They no longer needed to show him their monthly ticket; instead, they were part of the commuter in-crowd and could just gab and giggle.

"Well, I have an entire tidbit," Diana now said, "I have been banned from Rikers."

"Rikers?" Allen asked.

"Rikers Island Correctional Facility. They won't let me take my students to visit the inmates anymore."

"Do you know why?" Beverly asked.

"No clue," Diana responded. "But I'll call in a few chits and hopefully I can get back in. Otherwise, we can always take a field trip to Sing Sing prison." She didn't sound too concerned.

"I hope the train gets in on time this morning," Beverly said with a sigh. "I have an important meeting with a new client. First impressions are so important, and tardiness just doesn't cut it."

At fifty nine, Beverly was the baby of the group. She had long straight auburn hair, (which she proudly attributed to Nicole, her hairdresser), alabaster skin, bright blue eyes, and a mischievous smile. Although she was overly concerned with aging issues, she always looked like she'd rushed out of the house: hair pulled back in a ponytail, very little makeup, and in a frenzy most of the time. Beverly owned a successful boutique recruitment firm called Priceless Placements, which recruited and placed "creative types," as she put it. Diana believed that Beverly had become a recruiter because she always wants to fix things, or make them right. Placing the perfect person in the perfect job seemed to meet her needs. She also loved to push the envelope and have fun, which is why she was such a accomplished businesswoman. Risk was something that came easily to her.

* * *

As the train lumbered down the tracks, Tom entered the car to collect the tickets. The gang placed him around fifty years old. He was a bit rotund, standing over six feet tall, with wavy grayish brown hair. His perpetual scowl put most people off, but the gang knew from experience that a warm morning hello would force a smile from him.

This morning, Beverly decided to be a good commuter and show Tom her monthly ticket. "Where is it?"

"Where is what?" Diana asked.

"My monthly pass, where is it?"

"How would we know?" they all asked at once. Tom ignored the panic and kept walking. He trusted her.

"I'll have to rummage through everything tonight looking for it. I can't believe it! It's only the beginning of the month. This thing costs a fortune. I wonder if Metro-North replaces lost tickets."

"They must have a procedure for replacing tickets," Margie said. "Did you use a credit card to purchase it or a check?"

"I used a check. Here comes Tom again. Let me ask him." Tom meandered down the aisle as Beverly grabbed his arm, "Tom, help! What if I can't find my monthly? Will they replace it?"

"If it's stolen, you'd have to file a police report," Tom answered, as he continued to walk down the train. "Otherwise, it's almost impossible to get it replaced."

"Just buy a couple of round trips," Allen advised. "As long as Tom's the conductor, you should be okay. Buy some senior citizen ones—they're cheaper."

"Yeah, really," Beverly retorted indignantly. "Thanks. I don't think so!" She was already in a panic about her approaching sixtieth birthday. "Tom is my evening conductor, so this might work out. Let's keep our fingers crossed that I find my ticket tonight."

"Seriously, Bev, didn't you almost lose your ticket a couple of months ago?" Diana asked her forgetful friend. "I thought you found it in Ron's wallet. Remember?"

"What a memory you have. You're right. Tom was off that evening, and we had a different evening conductor. I'd just handed Ron my pass to show it to the conductor for me because I wanted to sleep. But I didn't come home with Ron last night, and Tom wasn't on the train again, so I had to show my monthly. I just can't remember where I put it. Is this what happens when you're about to turn sixty? Totally lose your memory?"

"Yes!" they all agreed and had a good laugh. Beverly calmed down as the gang sat back to read or sleep.

Diana rested her head against the back of her seat, closed her eyes and relaxed. Suddenly she jolted upright, went into her commuter bag and pulled out the Elizabeth Peters book that Beverly had given her earlier. Holding the book jacket open with both hands, she turned the book upside down and shook it. Out fell Beverly's monthly pass!

"Mystery solved," Diana said, smiling as the gang gave her a round of applause and Beverly a hug of gratitude.

"How'd you figure it out?" Beverly asked.

"You know I do my best work with a relaxed brain. I was just resting when my little grey cells as Poirot would say, realized that last night, when you knew you had to show your monthly, you must have taken it out and placed it in your book and then just forgot to put it back in your wallet. Deductive reasoning."

"So, now you're thinking like Poirot and Sherlock Holmes?" asked Margie.

"Why not? You know I'm a frustrated detective. This could be my most exciting case of the year."

"This'll probably be your *only* case of the year," added Allen.

* * *

The train was in the tunnel and approaching Grand Central Station. Commuters began to stand and bundle up in anticipation of the cold weather. The gang packed away their reading materials and made sure Diana had all-her-belongings, since she had a tendency to leave things behind. Diana's days were so logistically varied that she was often confused about what she was schlepping around. The gang instinctively made sure she left with all her paraphernalia, which ran the gamut from the mundane to the absurd. Once, she carried around a picture made of yarn that an inmate from the local prison had made for her; another time, she was loaded down with hundreds of crayons for a charitable event; perhaps her most absurd "schlep" was a phony elephant tusk she was using as a prop for a class lecture.

As they disembarked, the gang steered Diana in the right direction. As she would say, she was directionally challenged and 100 percent of the time ended up heading the wrong way. During the day, Diana was able to cope with her inability to navigate, but in the evening, she preferred to take someone with her who would actually get her to the correct destination without any unscheduled sightseeing.

The gang headed toward the main terminal where they split up and headed in different directions. Today Diana remained in the Graybar Building, where she kept an office away from campus to focus on her research without distraction. She loved these days because since the office building was attached to Grand Central, she didn't have to step outside and could stay warm and toasty. Margie headed down toward Wall Street,—though according to her, this was just a temporary headquarters. She was perpetually looking for office space in Midtown but had a terrible time actually deciding to rent. Diana believed Margie has gotten into the habit of "just looking" and would never move her office. Meanwhile, Bev had a two-block walk to Fifth Avenue while Allen worked a few blocks further down on Forty-fourth Street.

They grumbled as they approached their first flight of stairs to civilization. As they were saying their morning goodbyes, a man suddenly careened through the exit and barreled into Diana, pushing her from behind. She fell forward and toppled Beverly to the ground.

"What was that?" Diana gasped. "Are you all right?"

"Yes, sort of. Did you see who did that?" Beverly squirmed to freedom from under Diana's fur coat.

Margie and Allen had frozen and were staring speechless at the two women piled on the floor in their fur coats and looking like a cross between a coyote and a beaver. "Well guys, can someone give us a hand?," Beverly finally demanded as she sat up on the floor next to Diana, who was completely entangled in her coat, scarf, and bags.

A hand appeared in response to Beverly's plea for assistance. "Are you all right, ma'am?," asked a young soldier, who was part of the Homeland Security program. Since September 11, Grand Central Station was heavily guarded with police, soldiers, bomb-sniffing dogs, and no doubt many undercover agents, all of whom no doubt scared more people than made them feel safe, in Diana's opinion. Still, fears about terrorism had become a way of life, and you got used to almost anything.

"Yes, thank you, young man," Beverly said with deference.

The soldier bent down to help Diana gather her bags, then assisted her in standing. He left almost as quickly as he'd appeared, after talking into his headset. Diana assumed he was telling his superiors that he was helping some klutzy old biddies who'd fallen on top of each other and that there was no need to panic.

"Can either of you describe that guy?," Diana asked as she brushed herself off.

"I think I noticed him on the train, but I've never seen him before today," Margie said, finally finding her voice. "He was rather nondescript in a very ordinary way."

"He was probably just late for a meeting or something," Allen surmised. "That's why he didn't stop to see if you were okay."

"Don't be such an optimist—he was blatantly rude," Diana stated, rubbing her leg where it had hit the ground.

"Well, we can't waste anymore time hanging around here

lamenting over your woes," Margie said. "I have to get downtown." She started toward the subway.

"She's right," Bev said. "I have to hustle too."

The gang dispersed and went their separate ways without further incident.

CHAPTER 2

THE STRANGER FLEES THE SCENE

He kept running. "Those damn women, gettin' in my way. Well, they're not my concern, just typical rich broads from the burbs. I'm glad I ran them down. I'm already late. What happens if they think I'm not interested, that I've lost my nerve. This is too important to me."

The stranger weaved in and out of the crowds of commuters leaving Grand Central Station. He exited the tunnel and walked up Forty-second Street, heading toward the Westside. He began to run again, but he didn't want to arrive out of breath. He slowed down and began walking at a fast clip. He made every red light, and as he waited on the curbs for the lights to turn green, perspiration began to drip down his face. His entire body felt clammy.

"How can I be sweating, its sub-zero weather," he thought desperately.

He arrived at an Art Deco pre-war building, beautifully appointed, and only twelve stories high on West Forty-fourth Street. He entered, told the concierge he was expected on the sixth floor, signed in and grabbed the next elevator. The doors opened onto a well-lit elegant floor with thick, deep blue carpeting, deco light fixtures, and navy blue-and-beige striped wallpaper. He walked to the end of the hallway and turned the doorknob to Suite 605. In complete contrast with the rest of the building, the room he entered was stark, consisting of one long folding table surrounded by eight metal folding chairs. All the seats were taken except one. As he approached the empty chair, the man at the end of the table stared at him and said in an annoyed tone, "You're late."

CHAPTER 3

A POWER LUNCH—GANG STYLE

Diana, seated in her office, stared at her computer screen, still thinking about the morning's excitement. "I wonder if that rude young man will be on the train tomorrow," she pondered. "I can't believe he didn't stop to apologize and help us." As she rubbed her bruised leg, she turned her mind to her list of tasks for the day.

"So much to do, what to do first?" she pondered. She decided to check her emails; it had been a couple of hours since she'd last looked.

An email had arrived from Margie: "Have an appointment in Midtown to look at office space. Maybe the gang can meet at Chez Jacques for a leisurely, relaxed lunch, but I need to be back in the office by 1:30 p.m., so we have to redefine leisurely and relaxed. Just call my cell and let me know."

"Chez Jacques, oh yes. I need some of Jacques's cooking to cheer me up," Diana thought as she picked up the phone to call Beverly. "I ache all over from the fall this morning and need a reward."

"Beverly, I have two words for you—Chez Jacques! Lunch today, Margie is in Midtown. Please say yes. We are rewarding ourselves because we were brutally attacked today."

"A bit of an exaggeration, but you're on! Did you check with Allen?"

That's my next call. If you don't hear from me again, meet us there at noon. Margie only has a short window. Bye." Diana quickly hung up and dialed Allen.

"Allen, I know I can always count on you for restaurant company. The gang wants to meet at Chez Jacques for lunch today at noon. Say yes and then call Jacques and get us a great table."

"You're on! Just show up, he'll give us anything we want. After all, he's one of us—a commuter. See you soon."

Jacques, a master French chef, used to ride the train with the gang, but since opening the restaurant of his dreams three years ago, he commuted on an earlier train. So whenever the gang had an excuse to meet at his restaurant, Chez Jacques, they enthusiastically grabbed it—not only to see him but also to eat his fabulous food. Both Margie and Allen had known him for many years: Allen from commuting with him and Margie from taking some of the cooking classes he conducted periodically for various local charities. Diana and Beverly had been introduced to Jacques by Allen and Margie. He had become a great friend to them all and never refused them a meal.

Diana confirmed the lunch date with Margie via cell and finished Task Number Three on her list of five.

It was now 11:45 a.m., and Diana was lusting for lunch—until she remembered that she would now have to deal with the frigid weather. She bundled up again, exited the office building and headed for Third Avenue and Forty-fifth Street. Not a long walk, but enough to make her crave some hot soup. "I hope Jacques has some on his menu," she thought.

As she approached the restaurant, Margie disembarked from a cab, and Beverly turned the corner. As the three entered together, they saw Allen already sitting at "their table." The restaurant was small but very elegant, with murals of Paris adorning the walls. Diana loved their usual table because it was under the picture of the Tuilleries, one of her favorite spots in Paris. As the three women removed their coats, scarves, hats, and gloves, Jacques emerged from the kitchen to greet them.

"Bonjour, Jacques," the three greeted him. He hugged each of them, planting a kiss on both sides of their cheeks, and told them he had already placed their orders. Jacques always placed their orders—he dictated what they would eat because, after all, he was the chef! They deferred to him gladly.

Diana could not resist. "Soup, Jacques, soup, *s'il vous plait?*" she begged, with a big question mark at the end of her sentence.

"Of course, on such a day, only my best *soup de jour* to warm you up," Jacques responded. "My onion soup is *tres parfait*, and the bread has just come out of the oven. Henri will bring it to you immediately, while your main course is being prepared. Excuse me now, while I return to the kitchen."

"Well, have you two women recovered from your assault?" teased Allen.

"My leg hurts, and I know I'll be sore tomorrow," Diana complained. After all, I took the brunt of the fall."

"Are you delusional? You fell on me! I took the brunt of the fall, Beverly countered, holding back a major laugh. "You almost smothered me to death."

"Well perhaps I exaggerated," Diana conceded. "If this is the only thing in our lives we have to discuss, I guess we're in pretty bad shape."

"I wonder if we'll ever see that creep again?" Margie

contemplated.

"I think you're jumping to conclusions," Allen said.

"And what do you mean by that?" Bev asked with annoyance.

"Calling him a creep is a bit premature. Perhaps he didn't realize he toppled you two."

"Toppled us? Are we that fragile that we can be toppled?" Diana asked.

Before anyone dared to respond, Henri placed four bowls of wonderful aromatic onion soup in front of the gang. They each paused to absorb the warmth from their bowls and to inhale the smell of the onions and cheese.

The four started to slurp their soup with oohs and ahs as smiles appeared on their faces.

"I finally feel relaxed," Margie stated.

"What's wrong?" Diana asked with concern.

"It's Howie. I just want him to be happy and pursue his dream." Margie said, referring to her son.

"So, what's wrong with that?" Allen asked.

"Nothing, but his dream changes every day. Today an actor, tomorrow a doctor, and last week, he wanted to learn how to start a hedge fund! That's a bit of a reach, don't you think?"

Margie's motherly complaints were well founded since her son never paused long enough on one dream to make it a reality.

"Oh, I almost forgot," Beverly interjected. "I was so consumed with my monthly-ticket fiasco this morning, I *did* forget. Here, I found this on the Internet—but only follow through if Howie is actually still focused on his acting dream. A small troupe that puts on children's shows is looking for an actor who can sing. I think this might be perfect for him."

"Let me see that." Diana grabbed the paper out of Margie's hands.

"Absolutely, I agree," she confirmed after glancing at the paper, then passed the information back to Margie, who was glaring at her nosy friend.

Margie perused the ad. "Yes, yes, it does sound perfect for him, and, it appears to pay. I'll check this out and send in his resume." she said in her motherly voice.

"Just think, I may have landed him his first job. Do I get a commission?," Beverly teased.

"Well, of course," Margie said, sounding as if a cloud had been lifted from her head. Beverly had saved the day. The gang never let her down!

Just then Henri appeared, ready to serve the main course. The gang just looked over at the tray, eager to know what Jacques had selected for them. Diana, of course jumped right in and asked, "Henri, what is it? It smells divine."

A few moments later, Jacques joined them at their table. "*Mes amis*, I know how you watch your diet, and keeping that in mind, I am serving you *medaillons de saumon des canons de basel* with my special *beurre blanc* sauce."

"That sounds terrific, Jacques, but I studied Spanish for eight years," Diana said, teasing. "Translate, please."

Margie interrupted before Jacques had time to explain: "Salmon medallions old basel style with a white butter sauce."

"That is correct," Jacques said. "You have eaten this before, I remember now, and you loved it. I made this for you in one of my classes, oh, many years ago, *oui?*"

"Right! It hit the spot then, and I'm sure it will do the same now," Margie said as Henri placed the meal before her. "It looks delicious!"

Each plate was presented beautifully; the medallions of salmon were joined with a side dish of rice pilaf.

"Jacques is on the money," Beverly agreed. "Nothing could be better than having salmon with its healthy amino fatty acids."

"Except for one problem," Allen noted. They all stared at him in anticipation, "You may be more diligent and conscientious in what you eat, but Jacques can give me high-cholesterol steak anytime." They all laughed at Allen's rebelliousness and proceeded to taste the salmon. Again, they oohed and aahed as they inhaled the tasty and healthy food.

Between bites, Margie asked Allen, "Is your son Andrew still dating …?"

"I know what you're asking," Allen said with a sigh, "but he has a new one now."

"He does goes through girlfriends at a rapid rate," Beverly commented.

"Yeah, and he isn't getting any younger. He's up in his thirties already, never married. He claims he's ready to settle down, but he doesn't seem to give these women a chance. As soon as things look good, he's onto another one!"

"It doesn't appear he really wants to settle down," Diana surmised. "Maybe he really enjoys playing the field."

"Looks like it," Allen agreed.

"Do I have a girl for you," Beverly declared, sounding like Barbra Streisand in *Hello Dolly*.

"Wow, first you may get Howie a paying acting job and now you want to marry Andrew off. What can't you do?" Diana asked, smiling.

"Seriously, I know this really successful, attractive, and

wonderful young woman who may be just what he needs. Allen, ask him if he's interested, okay?" Beverly pressed.

"I'll have to wait until he gets rid of this one—give me a week," Allen said with a note of fatherly frustration.

Beverly just nodded. Before long, Jacques came out to see what the gang wanted for dessert. They all insisted on passing; after eating their amino fatty acids, they thought better of clogging their arteries with one of Jacques's famous desserts. All praised the lunch and paid the bill.

Satiated from their terrific lunch, the gang, said good-bye to Jacques and put on their respective heavy coats, scarves, hats, and gloves to once again face the afternoon cold. Allen and Margie walked out of the restaurant first. As Beverly and Diana joined them, they saw their friends staring at something across the street.

"What're you looking at?" Diana asked.

"That's him, that's definitely him," Margie stated emphatically.

"Who's *him*?" Beverly asked.

"The man who attacked you this morning."

The four stood with their eyes fixated on the man. He was in his mid-thirties, very thin, and around five feet eight. His hair was frazzled brown speckled with gray and white, and he wore large horn-rimmed glasses with very thick lenses. His nose must have been quite prominent because they could all see it distinctly from across the street. He had on baggy pants, sneakers, and a green down jacket. Margie maintained that it had to be him because of his distinctive hooked nose.

"That's definitely him," she asserted. "I would recognize that nose and messy hair anywhere."

"And no one else in New York has a large nose and messy

hair?" Diana asked sarcastically.

"I know it's him. I saw him. *You* were buried in coyote and beaver, remember?"

"Okay, you win."

While the women bickered over the identity of the stranger, Allen was staring at him intently. Suddenly he interrupted and asked, "What's he doing?"

"Since he's talking to a shish kebob vendor, I would assume he's buying a shish kebob," Beverly chimed in.

"No, look," Allen said emphatically. "He just passed him something and is now walking away without a kebob."

"Do you think he's a drug dealer? He really doesn't fit the stereotype," Diana stated knowingly.

"Well, it does look fishy," Margie said, then began to giggle uncontrollably as she blurted out between laughs,—"or keboby!"

They all stared at her, and then they too burst into contagious laughter.

Finally, Margie caught her breath. "But I can't stand here freezing much longer. I need to hail a cab and get back to work."

The gang dispersed, each heading back to work fully satiated. But as Diana walked slowly back to her office, she felt a knot in her stomach. She related it directly to the stranger who seemed to have just entered their lives.

"You're being silly," she thought, shrugged and entered her building.

CHAPTER 4

THE STRANGER BECOMES STRANGER

Diana stood on the train platform surrounded by a throng of commuters and started to grin as her mind wandered to the Statue of Liberty: "'Give me your tired, your poor, your huddled masses...'– well, tired, yes. Poor, that's open to interpretation. Huddled, definitely. Two out of three ain't bad."

"It's coming," yelled Allen from the back of the pack.

Diana turned and spotted him, "You just got here, didn't you? Your timing is impeccable!" Beverly and Margie had also just arrived because it was much too cold to linger on the platform.

As the Metro-North train rolled into the station and slowed to a halt, it became apparent that it wasn't going to stop on Diana's spot. It was way off its target, and the door opened about six feet away from her. By the time she shoved her way in, she could only secure three of the four seats she needed for the gang.

Margie and Allen joined her, and Beverly continued to walk until she found an aisle seat two rows down on the other side. Allen and Margie sat facing Diana who was seated next to a commuter she'd frequently seen before but had never met. He promptly pulled out his iPod, plugged it into his ears, and zoned out.

As usual, Beverly removed her coat and placed it in the overhead rack. She sat down, pulled out her *New York Times* and removed the sports section for Allen, waving it so he would get up to retrieve it. Allen rose, walked over to Beverly, took the paper from her extended hand and quickly returned to his seat.

Margie settled in, and Diana finally warmed up enough to take off her hat and gloves.

Margie glanced up and gasped out loud.

"What's wrong?" Diana asked.

Margie elbowed Allen. He was already buried in the sports page, reading about the latest acquisition of the Yankees, which Diana considered a great escape from the reality of sub-zero weather.

Allen jumped slightly, "What the…"

"Shh," Margie whispered, nudging him. "Look who Beverly sat next to."

Allen looked up, eyeing Beverly. Diana started to turn to look as well when Margie kicked her.

"Ouch," she whispered loudly. Margie signaled her to sit still.

Allen was smiling, almost giggling.

"This isn't funny," Margie said sternly. She pulled out one of her small pads of paper and wrote: "Beverly, stay calm, look left." Then she folded the paper and handed it to Allen.

"Act nonchalant, and pass this to Beverly," she instructed.

Allen nodded and slowly rose again from his seat, walking toward Beverly. He bent down and said to her, "This is from Margie. It's the information you asked her for yesterday."

Beverly looked at him quizzically but took the note. Allen

returned to his seat and picked up his paper, but he and Margie kept their eyes on Beverly. Diana, who had no idea what was going on, sat there seething. Margie leaned forward and explained in a whisper, "Beverly sat next to your attacker!"

Diana's mouth dropped open and her eyes widened, "What's she doing?"

Margie and Allen watched as Beverly looked left as instructed. When Beverly first opened the note, a look of alarm had crossed her face, her lips tensed, and she brushed her hair back, a telltale sign that she was nervous. But Beverly regained her composure quickly. She cautiously watched the stranger who was staring down at his cell phone while text-messaging oblivious to his surroundings. Beverly opened her large, brown leather bag—a bag that could hold enough paraphernalia for a weeklong vacation—and rifled around in it.

Margie observed Beverly as she glanced down at the LCD screen on the stranger's phone. As she watched her friend, Margie whispered to Diana and Allen, "Wow, I think Beverly is writing down what the stranger is reading on his cell phone. She's a great covert operative! It looks like she's just frustrated at not finding something in her bag."

"Well, I'm so glad you have such a great view of the action," Diana complained. "I'm dying of curiosity! Keep watching and if anything gets interesting, just tell me, okay?"

Margie just grinned at her nosy friend and nodded.

Margie continued her observations. The stranger had stopped text-messaging and suddenly turned off his phone. A few seconds later, it was apparent that Beverly had completed her task because she pulled her hands out of her bag and gave the gang a subtle thumbs up. The stranger now pulled out his laptop. Beverly glanced over to see what he was doing, but this appeared to be less interesting than his texting because Margie saw her friend close her eyes, pretending to sleep.

As the train pulled into Grand Central Station, Beverly jumped up and gathered her coat, then came over to join the gang before the train stopped. "Follow me and let's move quickly," she said urgently.

They wove in and out of the crowd until they were standing in the middle of Grand Central. Beverly whipped out her cell phone and dialed, "Good, you're there, is the coffee on? We'll be right over, let us in."

The other three just watched until she hung up. "Okay, fill us in, will you?" Diana demanded.

"We're going to Jacques's for breakfast. We need to powwow. I'll fill you in then. Let's hustle."

The gang walked over in silence. Diana was a bit apprehensive. She had never seen Beverly so unnerved.

* * *

The gang stood in front of Chez Jacques as Beverly knocked on the door. Suddenly it opened, and they all entered, cold and out of breath. Beverly had set the pace, and she had them all walking at marathon speed. Jacques greeted them in his wonderful French accent, "Two days in a row, too good to be true. What's the occasion?"

"Well, we have some time to kill and thought we'd warm up here," Beverly said awkwardly. Diana, a bit taken aback by how evasive Beverly sounded, just stared in disbelief at her friend.

Jacques, shrugged his shoulders. "Well, I would love to join you, but I have meals to prepare," he said. "Please take some coffee and croissants while I return to the kitchen."

"Thanks," the gang all seemed to say at once.

"Okay, what's going on?" Diana demanded. She was feeling totally in the dark about the events on the train and didn't like that feeling at all.

"Let's take off our coats and grab some coffee, and then Beverly can calmly tell us what she saw," Margie said in her level-headed way.

Once seated with hot coffee and croissant, Beverly took out her pad. "When Allen approached me with the note to look left, I was a bit rattled," she said, "but once I spied our stranger's text messages, I immediately thought it would be best to record them because they confused me. It took me a while to find a pen and my little spiral pad in my oversized and, needless to say, very messy commuter bag, but once I had it at the ready, I began writing down, and might I add, in lousy handwriting, what I could read off his screen. Our nerdy stranger was very busy texting on his phone. I love texting. I was able to read the dialogue he was having. Here, look at it."

They all bent over to read it. Beverly was right. It really was scribbled.

"Haman, next Friday RT?

Yes

7:20

As planned

The bridge

Awaiting instructions, be prepared—major blast"

"Well, I guess he now has a name," Diana observed.

"Yeah," Allen agreed, "Haman. He looks like a Haman."

The three women just stared at him.

"Well, he does," Allen insisted. "Don't you know the biblical story of Haman?"

The three women looked blankly at Allen. Suddenly, they all seemed to come to the same realization and understood what Allen was implying.

Beverly, "Purim…?"

Diana, "Queen Esther…"

Margie said very pensively, "Refresh my memory."

Allen took a deep breath and started telling the story of Haman. "Diana, you're right. The story of Haman is from the Book of Esther. Haman was a honcho to the Persian King."

"King Xerxes, and Haman was sort of his Prime Minister," Diana chimed in, recalling the Introduction to Jewish Holidays course she once took when she and Josh decided they needed to inject some religion into their daughter's life.

"Whatever. Anyway, Queen Esther is married to the King and no one knows she's Jewish. Haman got insulted when Esther's cousin, Mordecai, would not bow down to him as required by law. It appeared that Jews would not bow to Persian officials even though it was required. Well, Haman was furious, hated the Jews anyway, and arranged with the King to have all the Jews killed. Mordecai asked for intervention from Esther and to make a long story short…"

"No, tell the entire story." Diana insisted. "It may give us some needed insights And worst case, it's a refresher course in Purim."

"Okay," Allen said with a sigh. He took a deep breath and continued. "Esther asked the Jews to fast for three days, and then said she would ask the King to save her people. They all fasted, including the Queen. According to Persian law no one was permitted to approach the King, not even his Queen—he had to summon the person. Esther decided to break the law, knowing the King could have her killed for that transgression, and she waited for him. He held up his scepter, giving her permission to talk. She invited him and

Haman to dinner.

"Why dinner? asked Beverly "Why not just tell him what was going on?"

"Now, how would I know? This is just my limited memory, or as you would say, Diana, my little grey cells working, recalling the megillah readings and all of the Purim festivals I took my kids to. Some actually went as Haman. Of course, my daughter always went as Queen Esther...."

"My daughter did too," Diana said. "She was the cutest Queen Esther." Diana suddenly visualized her daughter in a costume made from a white pillowcase decorated with gold fringes and lots of costume-gold jewelry. "She had had the cutest headdress, also with ornamental pieces of gold."

"Let's get on with the story," Margie nudged. "We all have to get to work sometime today."

"Well, Haman was on cloud nine. He thought he was really in good with the King because the Queen liked him too. But in the interim, the King found out how loyal Mordecai had been to him by preventing his enemies from killing him. So he wanted to reward him. The Queen has a second dinner, at which time she reveals how evil Haman is and his impending plans to annihilate her people. The King storms out and goes for a walk. Haman literally throws himself at the Queen, begging for forgiveness. The King returns, sees him on top of the Queen, so to speak, thinks he's attacking her and has him killed. End of story. Remember, some of my details may be wrong, but the gist is correct."

"So to summarize, Haman is a true villain," Diana concluded. Her image of her daughter as Queen Esther faded away.

"What do you think this means?" Margie asked.

"It may mean nothing. It just might be his name," Allen said.

"Or not," Beverly said. "It may be a pseudonym."

"Well, there is no real way of finding that out unless he drops his wallet and we retrieve it," Margie noted.

"Fat chance. Let's just keep this bit of information aside for now and discuss the text message," Diana said pragmatically.

"Who wants to start?" Margie asked. "Beverly, you've had more time to digest it."

"Good point. I guess." Beverly paused.

"What?" Diana coaxed, hearing fear in her friend's voice.

"I was afraid it meant he planned on blowing up our train. That was my first reaction," Beverly whispered.

"But how can we even begin to guess?" Diana asked.

"Well, let's look at the facts. 7:20 is our train," Allen said.

"It is, but we get it at Westport at 7:20, and it originates somewhere else, north of us at a different time," Diana observed.

"Did Haman get on at our stop?" Beverly asked with a quiver in her voice. "He just can't be a Westporter."

"Why? No weirdoes live in Westport?" Diana asked and then felt guilty for upsetting her friend.

"Since we've never seen him before, maybe he's staying in Westport temporarily or just moved here," Margie ventured.

"Did anyone notice him standing near us on the platform?" Allen asked.

The three women shook their heads in the negative.

"I think we need to determine if he takes the train from Westport," Diana said matter-of-factly. "That's step one."

"Okay, what's step two?" Margie asked.

"That's tricky," Diana said. "Do you think he plans on blowing up the train over a bridge? And which bridge?"

31

"Well, if we accept the fact that this is a terrorist plot to blow up our train, it's a good guess it's some bridge on route to Manhattan," Allen said sarcastically.

"You think we're nuts, huh?" Diana asked.

"Well, I think we're getting carried away. The three of you have very vivid imaginations, and I'm just reining you in a bit," Allen said this in a fatherly tone.

"Is he a suicide bomber?" Margie asked in a panicky tone, needing clarity.

"Maybe he's just going to plant the explosives and get off the train at East Norwalk," Diana suggested. "And also, what's the significance of RT? Rush train, ruin train?"

"Renovate train, that would be nice," Beverly joked, trying to forget her fears.

"Beverly, this is no time to get a sense of humor," Diana said firmly.

"Sorry, couldn't help myself."

"We need a step two," Margie said nervously, trying to get everyone to focus.

"Okay, okay," Diana responded, thinking hard. Finally she said, "According to *Milespost*…"

"What are you talking about, *Milespost*?" Beverly asked.

"You know the Metro-North newsletter that appears occasionally on our seats. Anyway, according to *Milespost*,…wait a minute, I have it in my bag, let me get it out and read you the relevant parts." She rummaged through her bag, which, as usual, was packed with all sorts of items. "Here it is: 'Don't label a person suspicious based on ethnicity, race, color, or religion…'"

"Does that include nerds: a white man, late twenties, early thirties, and a nerd?" Margie sounded frustrated.

"Okay, so he doesn't fit the stereotype. Let me skim down. Here goes: 'Never approach a suspicious individual or tamper with suspicious packages; leave any action to specially trained police units. If you suspect something…alert a Metro-North employee or a train crew member, a police officer, or a member of the National Guard.' Oh, and it says no one will blame us for being cautious. Personally, since Allen thinks we're overreacting and we clearly don't want to look foolish, I think we should tell Tom, our conductor. We'd be keeping within the suggested guidelines, and we can do it informally, so we're not on the record if it turns out to be our runaway imaginations."

"Brilliant," the other three agreed in unison.

"Tom goes to Alfredo's after work for a drink before he heads home—I can get there in time and talk to him," Allen volunteered. He felt guilty for not sharing the gang's fear of imminent danger.

"No, we should all meet you at Alfredo's to tell Tom," Diana said. "Five heads are better than two."

"You just don't like missing out on anything," Margie said. "You're so nosy."

"Yes, I am," Diana said, "and I'm proud of it."

Beverly still looked scared. "This could be serious," she said. "Are we prepared to get involved in something this dangerous?"

"Yes, why not?" Diana said without hesitation. "We could be saving a lot of lives including our own!"

"Okay, okay, we all meet at Alfredo's tonight. What time, Allen?" Beverly asked.

"Tom is generally there by 5:30. I'll keep him occupied until you all arrive, and…I know…I promise not to tell him anything before you join us."

Allen got up to find Jacques and tell him they were leaving. The three women started to bundle up. Usually upbeat, they now all looked solemn and scared. Never a group to shy away from a challenge, the gang was entering into something they knew nothing about—unless Allen was right and it was probably nothing at all to fret about...or was it?

Allen joined the women as they left the restaurant. They instinctively looked across the street to see if Haman was there with the shish kebob vendor.

"Oh, no!" screamed Margie.

CHAPTER 5

SHISH KEBOB NO MORE

"What? What's wrong?" Diana yelled.

"I'm late! Howie's playing a willow tree, and I promised to be at the dress rehearsal. I'm late!" Margie hailed a cab, jumped in and was gone in a flash.

"A willow tree?" Allen asked.

"Yes, we've been so embroiled in our adventure that Margie forgot to tell you the good news. She contacted the acting troupe for Howie, pretending to be his agent and got him an audition late yesterday. They just fell in love with him, and now he's one of the stars of the troupe." Beverly beamed as his talent scout.

"Well, that's terrific, but she scared me to death with that yell of hers," said Diana. "Anyway, I've got to go and play professor."

"See you all tonight, I'm going to play recruiter," Beverly said with a laugh.

"I'm just off," Allen added, as they all parted, forgetting about the shish kebob vendor.

In a doorway across the street, near where the shish kebob vendor sets up his cart, a tall thin man in khaki pants and a dark black down jacket, with a black wool hat pulled way down on his face watched the gang as they left Jacques' and disbursed in all different directions. He then scanned the entire block going north, then south aware of all the pedestrians approaching and the traffic flow.

When all seemed clear, he diverted his attention from the daily traffic to the shish kebob vendor as he wheeled his cart to the corner. The vendor parked it in his usual spot, and began to set up his display. The corner was quiet. It was past rush hour and too early for lunch, so the vendor had time to set up and begin making his kebobs. Intent on his work, the vendor seemed unaware of his surroundings; the people and the traffic were just background as he focused on his chores. Very cautiously, the man in the doorway put his hand inside his jacket and slid out his Glock with a silencer on it. He looked around one more time to make sure the street was void of pedestrians, then in a flash pulled up the gun, aimed and shot the shish kebob vendor in the back of the head. The vendor died instantly and slumped forward over his cart. The stranger quickly returned his revolver to its holster hidden by his jacket, moved out of the doorway, turned away from the cart and walked quickly down the street. No one took notice as the killer easily escaped.

CHAPTER 6

TELLING THE TALE

Allen sat pensively on the 4:36 p.m. Metro-North train heading back to Westport. He was apprehensive about the meeting with Tom. "Was he the right person to talk to? Were they all being silly about Haman? Perhaps he was just an ordinary guy, no intrigue at all." Yet, he felt a gnawing in his stomach and knew it wasn't indigestion. He always got nervous when he embarked on something new that was not a part of his daily routine. Alice, his wife, always teased him about his "ruts," as she called them. But he knew this meeting was only going to open more doors that he just didn't want to enter. He loved his ruts!

The train pulled into the station. Allen zipped up his black leather jacket, walked across the street and entered Alfredo's Restaurant.

Alfredo's had been a Westport landmark for more than twenty years. It was a small Italian restaurant that attracted a wonderful cross section of the town's residents. You didn't have to be a commuter to hang out at Alfredo's. The restaurant was dimly lit with a handful of tables. The bar area was as large as the dining area and usually standing room only. There was always lively chatter as the patrons imbibed while waiting for a table.

As Allen opened the door, the warmth and aromas coming from the restaurant instantly relaxed him. This was one of his hangouts, so his visceral reaction was a welcome feeling after the angst he'd had all day. The bar was crowded with commuters who had stopped by for a drink before heading home, but Allen immediately spotted Tom seated at the bar. He sauntered over and gave him a slap on the back. "Want some company?" he asked.

"Have a seat, boss," Tom said with a rare smile. Ever since Allen had started hanging out with the gang, Tom always referred to him as "boss."

"Allen. Welcome, my friend," yelled Alfredo from the other end of the bar.

"I just couldn't stay away," Allen yelled back over the bar noise. He routinely dropped by every morning for coffee and an occasional breakfast and schmoozing before boarding the train, so it had only been a few hours since their last meeting.

"Second drinks on me," Alfredo generously offered.

"Yeah sure, you know I'm a one-drink guy." Allen responded, and they all laughed.

Allen slid next to Tom at the bar, and Nick the bartender placed a lite beer in front of him.

As Allen slowly raised his glass, Tom asked, "So what brings you here so early? I thought you usually go home first to pick up your wife."

"I think the gang is planning to drop by for a drink, and I promised to wait for them. They should be here any minute. They would love to say hi. Can you stay?"

"Sure," Tom replied glancing at his watch. "My wife has

decided to take up needlepoint and has a class tonight. She told me to fend for myself for dinner, so I'm just passing the time and waiting for the traffic to subside. Hanging out with you guys will be a nice break."

"Well then, this is a perfect night for some after-work schmoozing with Al's Girls." Allen was secretly thrilled that he didn't have to fabricate some lame excuse to keep Tom preoccupied until the gang appeared. "Why don't I see if Alfredo will give us a table, and then we can order an antipasto as a before-dinner *hors d'oeuvre*," he suggested. He thought this would give the group at least some privacy while they unveiled their story.

"I could use something to tide me over until I get to my local McDonald's for my main course," Tom said sarcastically.

"Wait here. Let me see if I can work some magic. The restaurant doesn't look as crowded as usual, so we might get lucky." Allen jumped off the stool and headed toward Alfredo, who was still standing at the end of the bar. Tom watched as Allen and Alfredo conversed; he saw Alfredo give a smile and a nod. Allen waved to Tom to join him. Tom weaved through the crowd at the bar to join Allen "This is your lucky day," Alfredo chided. "Allen persuaded me to take pity on a man orphaned by a needlepoint class and rescue you from a Big Mac. Follow me, men. I'll have my famous antipasto delivered to your table at once. I was informed that three lovely ladies, none of whom is Allen's wife, will be joining you, correct?"

"Funny man! Alice knows how important the gang of four is," Allen said, as he and Tom followed Alfredo to the rear of the restaurant and a table nestled in the corner. "Perfect," he thought. "No one will bother with us here, and none of my friends can really see me unless they are searching for me. So we might even get away without interruption."

"Alfredo," Allen said, "you know the gang. Please be so kind and send them back here when they arrive."

"Absolutely," Alfredo said with a smile as he headed toward the front of the restaurant.

Shortly after they were seated, a waiter brought out a huge platter of antipasto and a basket of homemade bread sticks. The platter contained Alfredo's famous green beans Fiesole, prosciutto, sliced veal, sardines, anchovies, and tomato chunks with the most delicious Italian olives this side of the Atlantic. Just as they were about to "dig in," they heard a shrill, "Stop!"

Tom and Allen looked up to see Margie, Diana, and Beverly standing over them, salivating. "We would have left you some," Allen swore.

"Uh, huh," groaned the three women as they all took their seats around the table. Alfredo had taken their coats and put them in his office for safekeeping, since there was no coatroom at the restaurant and Diana and Beverly were reluctant to hang their furs on a hook on the wall. They had important things to discuss with Tom and didn't want to be preoccupied with having to keep an eye on their outer garments.

As the women made themselves comfortable, Tom and Allen began to plate the antipasto and pass the servings around the table until everyone had a sampling.

"Tom, we have a confession to make," Diana announced, in her usual blunt and tactless way, "This was not an accidental meeting. We need to discuss something with you of a delicate nature and we want this conversation to be off the record."

"Diana, I'm not a reporter..." Tom began to say as Allen, Margie, and Beverly broke into laughter. Diana just glared.

"Okay, you smarty pants, someone else pick up where I obviously failed," she said..

Beverly continued, "Tom, what I think my dear fellow commuter is trying to say, is that we need to discuss something with you that may concern the train, and if we're making a mountain out of a molehill, so to speak, we don't want to make this official."

Tom looked confused. "In other words," he said, "leave Metro-North out of it because what you're going to tell me is, what, senseless? Unfounded? Stupid?" They nodded in agreement to all three scenarios.

"Okay," he agreed, "to put this back in perspective, this will definitely be off the record!"

"See!" Diana screamed triumphantly.

"Well, now that you have piqued my curiosity, get on with it," Tom said, a bit impatiently.

"Let's start at the beginning," Diana began. She went on to describe how they had first met Haman when he knocked her and Beverly to the ground, how Beverly had read the ominous text message, and how they had spotted him again with the shish kebob vendor. Beverly then handed Tom a typed copy of the message in case he needed to study it. As he was perusing it, Allen started to stutter, looking flustered.

"What's the matter?" Diana asked. "I know, you still think we're nuts."

"No, definitely not," Allen insisted as the women stared at him in amazement.

"Something very strange happened after I left you this morning which convinced me that perhaps we *have* stumbled onto some plot to blow up the train—or who knows what, maybe something worse." He glanced around the table and noticed the worried expressions on the gang's faces and the look of concern on Tom's face.

"Well, what happened?" Diana asked.

"I guess I should also start at the beginning. After we met for breakfast at Jacques's, I decided to walk across town to my office. I know it was really cold, but the air felt good, and I find that a brisk walk can be invigorating. Besides, I had eaten three croissants."

"Allen, I realize that you don't want to leave anything out, and you did say you were going to start at the beginning, but can you try to get to the point a bit faster?" Diana coaxed.

"I was just trying to set the scene. Be patient, I'm getting there. So, as I was saying, as I approached my office building I could not believe what I saw."

"Don't tell me you saw the shish kebob vendor?" Beverly asked.

"Will you all please stop interrupting me!" Allen screamed.

It became apparent to all of them that Allen was stressed and quite upset. "We're very sorry, Allen," Diana said calmly. "Please continue."

"Thank you." Allen paused to set the scene again. "I thought I was seeing things. Haman was leaving my building. I instinctively looked at my watch to mentally record the time. It was 9:35 a.m. I thought that this was getting too weird—suddenly this guy was everywhere!"

The gang gasped but fearful of saying anything to further upset Allen, no one said a word. They just waited for him to continue. Tom listened intently.

"I asked Harry, the concierge in my building, who Haman was visiting. Naturally, I didn't use his name, I just described him. I know, I'll move it along. Anyway, all he knew was that Haman had gone to the sixth floor. He let me look at the sign-in sheet. There was no one named Haman. I did notice that a John Smith had signed in at 8:50 for the sixth floor. He hadn't written down which office, but at least that narrowed it down to a specific floor. So I decided to be daring and do a little investigating on my own. Diana, I know you would have been proud of me. I took the elevator to the sixth floor to peruse the offices and see if something popped out. The hall was deserted so I didn't feel conspicuous about just meandering around. I walked down the corridor, glancing left, then right, as each office door appeared, making mental notes about every tenant. I was beginning to think this was a silly exercise and that we were just alarmists in need of some excitement when I glanced up at the next door. As I stood in front of the door, I felt a knot in my stomach. That's when I immediately reassessed the situation. It was worse than I could've ever imagined."

There was a moment of silence. Finally, Diana couldn't help it and blurted, "So, tell us, what's on the floor?"

"A mosque," Allen stated matter-of-factly.

"A what?" the three women asked in shock.

"You heard me, a mosque. You remember me telling you about the mosque in my building. I forgot that it was on the sixth floor until I was face-to-face with it. If Haman was visiting the mosque, this could really be a very organized terrorist attack with substantial funding to make it succeed."

"So that's why you're a convert to our conspiracy theory," Diana said.

"Yep," Allen said, nodding. "This has had me really unnerved all day."

During Allen's revelation, Tom had remained silent, listening to the dialogue while astutely watching the four interact.

"I think perhaps it's now my turn," he finally interjected. The four turned to face him, mumbling in agreement. "You were absolutely correct to discuss this with me 'off the record.' I'm not really sure which passenger you are referring to, and from your description he seems fairly nondescript, anyway. I'll try to locate him tomorrow on the train. We may even get lucky and he'll be in your car. Now, what other types of offices are on the sixth floor? Could he have had a doctor's appointment, for instance?"

"Well, there was one doctor's office on the floor," Allen said. "but remember, he signed in as John Smith. That's an alias if I ever heard one."

"Point taken, but there could be a variety of reasons he may have used an alias. He might not want anyone to know he has some sort of disease…"

"Now you just wait a minute," Beverly reacted indignantly. "I sat next to him. I just hope he doesn't have some sort of contagious disease…"

"Oh Beverly, stop being an alarmist," Margie told her. "You're on the train with hundreds of people each day. I'm sure some of them are contagious."

"You know what? I think you folks may be able to help me. Allen, do you know anyone affiliated with the mosque?" Tom asked.

"Like the imam, or whatever?" Allen asked.

"Yes, so that you could get access to the mosque and check it out."

"Tom, you want me to pray at the mosque? Me, a Jew?" Allen was flabbergasted.

"No, not pretend to be a Muslim, but perhaps you can express an interest in Islam, a natural curiosity, and the imam will let you observe. You are a great schmoozer. Get access, check it out, and see if your Haman shows up."

"And what will you be doing in the mean time?" Margie asked.

"First, I want to take a look at this guy and see if he's on any lists," said Tom.

"What kind of lists?" Diana asked.

"We have a variety of watchdog lists, suspects, types of people, etc. Let me do some snooping on my end. I don't want any of you to get involved except for Allen and the mosque. And Allen, keep your snooping to a minimum, and if you see this Haman fellow, report it to me. Don't do anything else. Understand?"

"How come he gets to snoop and we don't?" asked Beverly. Since she'd written down Haman's message, she was sure she had what it took to be a spy.

"Because if there's something going on, we need to leave it to the professionals," Tom said. "I'm leery about filing a report until we have more evidence, so let me do my thing. I know what I have to do. You just keep observing and report anything and everything you see that seems suspicious. When Beverly was able to write down the text message, that was very important. That was good work. Don't take any chances and remember to tell me everything."

"Actually, I've talked with some of the men praying in the mosque," Allen said. "We've ridden the elevator together. They'll recognize me. This won't be too difficult. Good idea, I could get into this. I always wondered what went on in a mosque…" Allen was babbling.

Tom sat back and smiled at the gang. He hoped he had put them on the wrong track and could keep them preoccupied while he finished his job.

CHAPTER 7

THE ELEVEN O'CLOCK NEWS

Diana sat in Beverly's car, waiting for the heat to crank up. They had just left Alfredo's and Beverly had offered Diana a lift home. She shivered, knowing she would have to wait until she was home before she could actually warm up again.

"Well, did we do the correct thing by talking to Tom?" she finally asked as Beverly pulled out of her parking space.

Beverly gave it some thought. "We really didn't have a choice," she said. "I think he'll follow up. Anyway, he was quite insistent that we tell him about anything we think is suspicious, so he must've thought our findings had some merit."

"You're probably right. I just hope he wasn't humoring us," Diana mused as Beverly pulled into her driveway. She waved goodbye as she left the car . "See you tomorrow,—and thanks for the lift!"

* * *

Diana was snuggled in bed, her husband snoring in the background, as she surfed stations to hear the eleven o'clock news.

After Alfredo's, the remainder of her evening had been uneventful. Josh was at a business meeting until nine o'clock, so she ate a light dinner and folded some wash while watching mindless sitcoms.

She had turned on the news only to hear the next day's weather report, hoping for a break in the cold spell. and was just fading into a light sleep when she heard the anchor say, "A shish kebob vendor was found shot to death over his cart on Third Avenue and Forty-fifth Street. There appear to be no witnesses."

Diana sat up with a start and screamed, "Oh my ..."

"What, what's the matter?!" Josh jumped up startled.

"The shish kebob vendor was murdered," Diana moaned.

"Yeah, whatever, go back to sleep!"

"Fat chance," Diana thought. She realized that this news was very serious, very serious indeed. She hoped that the gang could handle yet another powwow tomorrow at Jacques's.

CHAPTER 8

THE SPY GAME—PART I

Diana dragged herself out of bed. She was shocked when her radio blasted the results of the Knicks game. "Why do I even care about sports? I should set my alarm for another time and another story. But then how will I shock my husband with my unusual knowledge of sports results and team standings?" She went through the motions of getting ready, but every part of her body ached with the fact that she had gotten very little sleep; she'd tossed and turned all night thinking about that poor shish kebob vendor. She knew exactly what she was going to do—but first she would discuss it with the gang.

* * *

Diana gave Josh a quick peck on the cheek and exited the car. She was standing shivering on the platform when Beverly joined her at the spot.

"You look terrible," Beverly said.

"Yeah, thanks, I had an awful night's sleep, to be discussed at Jacques for breakfast," she replied.

"Really?" Beverly asked, ready to jump into playing detective again.

"Really, no more discussion now," Diana said firmly.

"Fine."

Allen showed up on the platform with Margie right behind him, huffing and puffing, running late as usual. They all looked at each other and then simultaneously started to examine the platform for Haman. The train startled them as it pulled up to the station, catching them unawares. Just as the door opened, Diana glanced to her right and saw Haman enter their car through the front door. She was so shocked that she stumbled and almost fell down. Beverly quickly pulled her up by her scarf, gagging her.

"What are you doing?" Diana gasped.

"Saving you," Beverly countered.

"Well, thanks, but you're really defeating the purpose if you strangle me to death first," Diana said, rubbing her neck as she barreled inside and grabbed their four seats.

Once they were all comfortable, Diana glanced toward the front of the car and saw Haman sitting toward the middle. She pulled out a pad and wrote a note to the gang telling them she'd spotted Haman.

"Where's Tom?" Beverly asked.

"He hasn't appeared yet—stay calm," Margie urged.

"I have an idea, just a minute," Beverly said as she rifled through her huge bag. "I found it. Just stay cool."

"We're cool," Allen assured her.

Beverly took out her cell phone and positioned herself to make a call.

"Now is not the time to make a phone call," Diana stated in a hushed but frantic whisper.

"I'm not making a call, just pretending," Beverly asserted. "I want to take his picture with my new cell phone."

"Wow, when did you get that?" Diana asked.

"Last week. And yes, I didn't report in and tell everyone, okay?" Beverly said defensively.

"Okay, you're allowed to get a new phone without our permission." Diana sounded insulted.

"How will you position yourself to take his picture?" Margie asked. Riding backwards, she was unable to see Haman and was being really good about not turning around to try.

"I'm not sure, and since I've never really used this feature, I'm not sure it will even work," Beverly said, sounding uncertain.

"Give me your phone," Diana said. "I'll help you figure it out."

"You're no Ron," Beverly stated dismissively.

"Don't be such a smart aleck." Diana retorted. "I have the same phone, I can help you."

"I just assumed that if I had a problem, I would ask Ron. He's the technical one."

"Then I suggest you call him," Allen said. He assumed this discussion would go on forever unless he interceded.

"How hard can this be? Let me try first," Beverly said. She sounded like she was trying to convince herself. She got up and walked toward the doors of the train where polite commuters go to make phone calls to avoid disturbing the other passengers.

Diana, Margie, and Allen watched her as she very adeptly pretended to make a phone call and seemed to snap a picture. She looked down at the phone and turned to them with a look of horror.

She was clearly panicking and stood frozen, staring at the phone.

"Beverly?" Diana whispered from where they sat. "Beverly, are you okay?"

"Yes," she answered, "just give me a second." She took a deep breath and pretended to make another phone call. This time, she gave them all a subtle thumbs up and proceeded to pretend to end her call. She turned and walked slowly back to her seat.

"Well, what happened?" Diana asked.

"I'm not sure I want to tell you. You're going to laugh and tease me about my lack of technology skills." Beverly was clearly embarrassed.

"We promise, no teasing," Margie assured her.

"I, I, I…," Beverly stuttered and looked down.

"You never get flustered. What happened?" Diana coaxed her friend.

"I, I took a selfie," she blurted out.

The gang knew how sensitive Beverly was, and they really didn't want to upset her, but they couldn't help it: They burst out laughing uncontrollably.

"You're making a scene, and now I feel really stupid—but I did get a great picture the second time. And don't ask to see the selfie or the picture of Haman, as I was supposed to be making a phone call. Where is Tom?" she asked in a worried tone. He needs to see this picture?"

"I hate to say this, but I didn't recognize his voice over the PA system," Allen said. "I think he's off today."

"He didn't say that last night. Don't you think he would have said something last night?" Margie asked with concern.

"Listen, let's not talk anymore," Diana implored. "I have

some news I have to share with you. Beverly, can you make a real call and ask Jacques if we can impose on him for another breakfast?"

"Sure, that's the easy part of this phone," She returned to the doors of the train and dialed the restaurant. She spoke for only a minute and returned with a smile.

"Not a problem, but Jacques has decided to give us a real breakfast. He's working on a new recipe for some sort of quiche. I was unable to understand his French, but I said we would be his guinea pigs, anyway. How bad can it be? It's a Jacques dish, right?"

"Right," they all chimed in.

"What's Haman doing now?" Margie asked

"He appears to be using his phone to text," Beverly said. "I wish I had sat down next to him. This is very frustrating, not being able to spy on him."

"Seriously, we need to stop talking about this here, please," Diana begged as the conductor—not Tom—stopped by their seats. Today's conductor was Mike, who shared the train-conducting job with Tom. The gang rarely saw him because he was assigned to the other half of the train. Mike was Tom's opposite: He had blond hair, blue eyes, and a gregarious personality.

Diana, Margie, and Beverly rifled through their purses and showed Mike their tickets. Allen, of course, knew Mike and got away with a warm greeting and infectious laugh.

"What should I do with the picture?" Beverly asked after Mike walked down the aisle.

"Okay, when you get to the office, call Ron and ask him how you can email the picture to yourself," Diana, instructed. "Then do it, print it out and make a couple of copies. We'll give one to Tom when we see him next, and I want one too. And now, can we stop talking about this here!" She was afraid someone would over hear their conversation.

They all stared at her, then nodded. Beverly passed Allen the sports page, Diana and Margie opened their books, and Beverly began reading the paper. They all pretended that this was just another workday.

As their train pulled into Grand Central Station, Diana leaned over and whispered, "Let's keep our eyes on Haman and see in which direction he goes. I know we can't follow him today, but if he heads toward Allen's building, that may be helpful. I think we should plan on following him one of these mornings."

"Stop talking!" the three of them said in unison as the rest of the passengers in the area stared at them.

Feeling a bit self-conscious, they quietly put away their reading materials and prepared to meet the cold weather. As the doors opened, they quickly pushed their way out, looking for Haman. Margie spotted him, elbowed Allen and pointed. Diana and Beverly, who were ahead of them, spotted Haman at about the same time. Diana began to weave through the crowd as only a native New Yorker can and came up behind him. His backpack looked quite full and made him slouch over. Diana wondered what he had in it. "Hopefully, just books," she thought.

Most of the commuters departed the platform and began climbing the steep stairs that led to a ramp that finally brought them into the Grand Central atrium. That had been Haman's route the day he pushed Diana and Beverly down. But today, he kept going straight toward another exit. Diana became flustered and stopped dead in her tracks, not knowing what to do.

"Hey, lady, what're ya doing, tryin' to kill us?" a commuter yelled as he almost knocked her down together with the people in front of her.

"I'm so sorry, I thought I left something on the train and panicked. Please forgive me," Diana apologized, saving the moment.

The gang caught up to her. "What do you think you were

doing?" Beverly asked as they all climbed the stairs.

"I froze," Diana said. "I just didn't want to lose him, and I knew we had decided not to follow him. I was torn." She sounded frustrated.

"We need to powwow, let's go," Margie said, leading them out of Grand Central as they began their cold trek towards Jacques's.

CHAPTER 9

A BREAKFAST BRIEFING

The gang stood in front of Chez Jacques, and Beverly knocked on the door. Francois, the sous chef, greeted them, "*Bonjour, bonjour, mes amis.*"

"Bonjour, Francois," they said as they marched inside, heaving a sigh of relief when the warmth in the room hit their cold and icy faces. This was an unusually windy morning, which, as the meteorologists would say, added dramatically to the wind-chill factor.

They peeled off their outer garments as Jacques came to greet them.

"As promised, I have created a wonderful breakfast quiche," he told them. "I am looking forward to your reaction."

"Well, French quiche is not exactly on any Weight Watcher list, Jacques. Are you trying to add to our girth?" Diana teased.

"No, no, that's the point. I think I have created a wonderful, nutritious, and low-fat quiche. Please, sit. Have some coffee, and I will have it brought out to you."

The gang helped themselves to the coffee and got

comfortable around the table.

Diana decided it was time for her to take control. "We have something important to discuss," she began.

"Well, yeah, we have a ton of things to discuss," Beverly interjected.

"Listen, I understand that, and we also have to be extra cautious about our conversations on the train. I'm afraid someone will overhear us, and who knows where that could lead? Anyway, Margie would you do me a favor and take a few notes? Just a list of things that we discuss and need to respond to," Diana asked, taking advantage of Margie's organizational skills.

"Certainly, just let me get that trusty pad of mine out of my bag. Ah, here it is. Shoot."

"Did any of you watch the eleven o'clock news last night?" Diana asked. They all shrugged and mumbled that they hadn't.

"Well, you'll never guess what one of the lead stories was…"

"A terrorist attack on a train?" guessed Beverly.

"No, no, no. The shish kebob vendor, the one from across the street…" Diana began when a giddy Margie interrupted…,

"Choked on a kebob?" Margie joked.

"And what if I said yes?" Diana asked with a straight face. As she sat back in her seat, she watched the gang trying to decide if she, too, was joking. She finally decided to put them out of their confused misery, "He was shot to death on the corner yesterday morning. There were no witnesses. It seems it happened right after we left here yesterday."

Margie, Beverly, and Allen stared at Diana, eyes wide and mouths open. Allen finally broke the silence.

"Are you certain it was our shish kebob vendor?" he asked with concern.

"It appears so. They gave the address as the corner across the street. How many shish kebob vendors do you think use that corner?"

"So, the plot thickens," Margie pondered aloud.

"I wonder if it's just a coincidence or if it has something to do with Haman?" Allen said.

"We need to start documenting all of our previous observations and going forward," Diana said. "Especially since Tom wanted to know about anything suspicious."

"Good point, I'll start the list right now," Margie said as she began to record the events.

"I've got a plan," Diana stated forcefully.

"Don't keep us in suspense," Beverly prodded. "You've obviously been contemplating this since last night, so out with it."

"Here goes. You know how involved I am with some members of the police department? They've been very helpful when I need advice and information for my students. Well, I'm friendly with a lieutenant at the One-Four. I know if I asked him, I could get some of the inside scoop on the murder of the shish kebob vendor. We need to find out why he was killed and perhaps who the suspects are, if they have any. I'll use my class as an excuse and ask if we can highlight this case as an example of how a homicide investigation is done. I know that Joe Venedri, that's the lieutenant, will tell me he can't give out any information on an ongoing investigation, but I may be able to get something out of him as he rejects my idea. He'll take pity on me."

"That sounds like a good place to start," Allen said. Margie and Beverly nodded in agreement.

"Next on our agenda," Diana kept going. "I want to go with Allen to visit the mosque. I know two sets of eyes are better than one and I know just how I'll get in."

Despite the seriousness of their discussion, the three other gang members started to laugh at Diana's statement. Some would call her meddlesome, others inquisitive. Needless to say, it all ended the same way—she refused to be left out.

"And how do you propose to get in? Dressed like a Muslim man?" Allen almost choked on his coffee as he imagined it.

"No, as myself," Diana asserted. "Sometimes the truth is the best vehicle."

"So, you're going to knock on the door of the mosque, tell the imam that you suspect a member of his congregation is a terrorist and you just want to have a look around to see if he's there?" Beverly tried to keep a straight face.

"Not exactly," Diana assured them. "I'll tell him that I'm teaching a section on terrorism in my criminology class and that I want to educate my students about the stereotypes that have developed around Islam. I want to learn more about what it's really about and help reduce the fears that are associated with Islam and specifically the American Islamic movement. I'll say that I think learning more about what occurs in an American mosque might be helpful."

"And that's being truthful?" Margie asked.

"Um, sort of. I do teach criminology, but that may put him off. I'll just say it's for my sociology course."

"Let's say you can get away with that. Do you really think they would let a woman inside?" Margie asked.

"I've seen women going into the mosque," Allen said pensively.

"See, not such a big deal, right?" Diana said, her voice hopeful.

As the gang of four pondered her proposal, Henri emerged

from the kitchen carrying the quiche. Jacques had made four individual quiches, and the aroma of the cheese, eggs, and whatever else he had put in was simply delectable. The four turned their attention to the food, enjoying their first bite.

"This doesn't taste like a low-cal quiche," Margie observed as she swallowed.

"I wonder what he made it with to reduce the fat and calorie count?" Diana asked, knowing no one could or would respond.

Just then Jacques appeared and looked at them inquiringly.

"We all agree, this is terrific and doesn't taste low calorie," Allen summed up for the gang.

"You're not just saying that to appease me, *n'es pas?*" Jacques asked.

"We really mean it," Diana assured him. "It's scrumptious."

Jacques wore a broad, handsome grin as he breathed a huge sigh of relief. "I have been working on this recipe for over six months," he said. "I want to change the content of my recipes to adjust to today's concern for healthy eating without compromising the taste. I am so glad that I have succeeded with the quiche."

"Jacques?" Diana interrupted his speech. "Did you ever notice the shish kebob vendor that sets up his cart across the street?"

"Shish kebob vendor? Across the street? Me? I do not associate with that level of 'cook.'"

"Don't take offense," Margie chimed in, "it seems he was murdered yesterday and we're just curious. We used to see him on the corner when we'd leave your restaurant, that's all. Just curious."

"You say he was murdered yesterday? Ah, yes, there did seem to be a lot of police activity on the corner, but I was so busy I didn't take time to investigate. I'm sorry. Should I have?" Jacques asked.

"No, as we said, we're just curious," Beverly added.

"Well I'm glad you're enjoying the breakfast. It's my treat since you're my testers! Back to the kitchen. Enjoy." Jacques left the gang and they returned to their discussion.

"That was a great idea you had, asking Jacques," Beverly said.

"We have to start snooping around a bit. That's the only way we'll find out anything," Diana confirmed.

"Excuse me, I don't mean to interrupt you…" Henri was standing next to the table. The gang all looked up at him, unaware of how long he'd been there.

"Yes, Henri," Allen said.

"I could not help but overhear what you asked Chef. You know, about the shish kebob vendor."

"What about the shish kebob vendor?" Diana asked excitedly.

"Well, sometimes when I'd go outside to take a smoke and get some fresh air, I'd walk across the street to chat with him," Henri said. "His name was Charlie."

"Do you know anything else about him?" Beverly asked.

"Only that he had three young children—one is very sick. He made kebobs during the day and drove a cab in the evenings. He was always complaining that he never got to see his children and never had enough money for them, especially the sick one."

"Do you have any idea who might have killed him?" Diana asked.

"No, I really never talked to him about much, just his family worries and the soccer scores."

"Soccer?" Diana pondered. "Was Charlie an American or was he born somewhere else?"

"I don't know," Henri said. "He sounded American to me. He just liked soccer, I guess. Excuse me, but I must go back to the kitchen. If I remember anything else, I'll be sure to tell you."

"Thanks Henri," Diana said. She turned to the group. "Well, we learned one fact about the shish kebob vendor: He needed money. Margie, that's a really important point. Write it down! And add his interest in soccer as well."

"Consider it done," Margie confirmed.

"Now, onto another point," Diana continued.

"There's more?" the three asked almost in unison.

"Well, just one small point. Where was Tom today?"

"I guess we would all like to know that," Allen said.

"Beverly," Diana said, "try to get the picture of Haman printed. You did a great job figuring out how to take his photo with your phone—even if it took two tries," she teased—"but I would like to show the picture to Lieutenant Venedri. If you bring it tomorrow, I'll scoot over to the precinct and try to kill two birds with one stone: try to get the scoop on the shish kebob vendor and the identity of Haman."

"Consider it done," Beverly said, "but I just want you all to know that I love my selfie."

"Of course you do," Diana said, grinning.

The gang finished their breakfast, said a quick goodbye to Jacques and left the restaurant. Out of habit, they glanced at the corner where the shish kebob vendor had worked. It was empty. They said their goodbyes and each headed to work.

The corner wouldn't be vacant long; after all, this was prime New York real estate. The shish kebob vendor would be replaced with a pretzel vendor that very morning.

CHAPTER 10

TOM TAKES IT TO ANOTHER LEVEL

Tom walked down the dimly lit corridor, head hanging, deep in thought. As he approached the office door, he sighed and walked in determinedly. He nodded at the workers seated at their old, peeling metal desks, all intently staring at their computer screens. He marched down the center aisle between the rows of desks toward the Commander's office door at the rear of the room. As he stood in front of the door, he wondered how the Commander would react to his information. He and the Commander were like oil and water and he never knew when he just might get "the boot."

He knocked and heard a gruff voice order, "Come in."

Tom entered and faced his Commander, a man in his early forties, with bags under his dark brown eyes and deep creases on his scowling face, seated behind a desk stacked with piles of papers. He was wearing a crumpled white shirt with rolled-up sleeves and no tie.

"Well, it's about time you showed up to give me an update," the Commander said with annoyance in his voice.

"I've been very busy, as you can well imagine," Tom said

defensively, "I need to discuss a slight glitch…"

"What do you mean, 'a slight glitch'? You assured me that everything was under control." The Commander clenched his teeth, clearly restraining himself from verbally exploding.

Tom slowly sat down and continued, "There are four commuters on the morning train…"

"And this is relevant to our plans?" he interrupted.

"Just let me finish, and you decide its relevancy." Tom paused a moment and went on when he felt he had his boss's attention. "Anyway, these four commuters have stumbled onto the plot to blow up the train…"

"Wait a minute. What is to decide? Of course this is relevant. How did they discover the plot?"

"That's a long story, and the details are in my report that I emailed you this morning. But the bottom line is that they intercepted a text message on Haman's cell phone and concluded it was a plan to blow up the train. They're very clever busybodies and are enjoying their roles as amateur sleuths. I think I got them off the scent. They trust me and will keep me informed about what they see and hear. I really believe I can keep them running around in circles and away from interfering with our plans. Hopefully, they'll get bored and move onto something else to keep themselves occupied." Tom sounded like he was trying to convince himself as well as the Commander.

"Tom, it's crucial to focus on our mission. You're our key operative, and your role is vital to the mission's success. We must take care of the train. Are you sure you have this under control?"

"I have everything under control. All operatives are in place, and we're ready to move as soon as we get the signal."

"Good, just take care of your 'glitch.' You don't need distractions right now or any screw-ups!"

"I will." Tom rose from his seat and exited the office. The Commander had made himself perfectly clear, but he could handle this. "I've handled much worse," he thought as he left the office.

CHAPTER 11

THE ARMANI CLUE

Diana stared out her large kitchen window as she sipped her morning coffee and watched the snow accumulate on her deck. Not only was it cold, it was also snowing—again! She knew she would have no trouble getting into the city, but if the snow continued to pile up, it would be a crapshoot getting home. Well, she wouldn't worry about that now; today was her teaching day, so she could leave the city early. She did have plans to visit Joe Venedri at the One-Four this morning on her way to school; hopefully, he would be there.

It appeared that the snowstorm had dissuaded many of the usual commuters from going into the city, and Diana had no trouble securing the gang's four seats. They were all present and accounted for. As they got comfortable, Margie leaned over and whispered, "He's here."

"Keep an inconspicuous eye on him," Diana said in a controlled voice. "Hopefully, Tom will be here this morning." She wanted to turn her head to snatch a glimpse but knew Margie would kick her again if she did. "Pavlovian conditioning is amazing," she thought.

"I have the photo you wanted," Beverly said.

"Great, can I have my copy?" Diana asked. "I'm heading for the One-Four right now."

Beverly held it up. "Here," she said, but Margie grabbed it first.

"I'm pulling a Diana," she said, chuckling as she took a long, hard look. "You took a really good photo. Was it difficult to download it to your computer to make the print?" She handed the photo to Diana.

"Piece of cake!" Beverly said confidently.

"Ron did it, right?" Allen asked, glancing up from the sports page Beverly had routinely handed him once they were seated.

The gang all started to laugh as the nearby commuters glared at them.

"So what, I completed my assignment. Not everyone is technical," Beverly said.

"She's right," Diana said. "She followed through and got the job done. It was a miracle that she was able to get the photo, so let's not press our luck. We should be thrilled we have Ron."

"A miracle? A miracle?" Beverly quickly changed the subject. "What's Haman doing now?"

"He appears to be sleeping," Allen reported.

"Here comes Tom," Margie said a bit too loudly.

"Shh," Diana whispered.

"Sorry," Margie apologized. "I'm just excited that he's here today. I got carried away."

"Hi folks," Tom called out, greeting them as usual.

"Tom, I have a photo for you," Beverly said, whispering carefully but clearly proud of her achievement. I took it yesterday with my cell phone. It's Haman. I made a copy for you so you could find out more about him."

"Let's see it," Tom said, sounding a bit peeved. He glanced at the photo. "Is he on the train?" he asked.

"Yeah, you just woke him up to look at his ticket," Allen said. He was a bit confused by Tom's sudden lack of memory.

"Oh, yeah, he's down the aisle. That guy. He looks harmless, if you ask me, a bit nerdy. I know, I promised to check him out for you," he said unconvincingly.

"Where were you yesterday?" Diana asked bluntly.

"I had a run-in with my boss and never made it in on time. Not a big deal, but we just don't seem to get along." Tom clearly did not want to engage the gang in any more conversations and continued to move down the aisle checking tickets.

Allen put down the paper, and the gang just looked at each other, bewildered.

Diana broke the silence. "Don't you think that was a bit odd?" she asked, leaning forward and whispering to the others.

"Yeah, he didn't associate the photo with Haman. It was like he never saw him before," Margie said, seeming to be talking out loud to herself.

"And he appears to be a disgruntled employee," Beverly noted, always the trained recruiter.

"Margie, pull out your pad and jot down those two points," Diana directed. "You never know when we might need to refresh our memories about the details."

"It seemed as if he'd lost interest in what we told him at Alfredo's. I wonder what went on between him and his boss?" Allen said.

"Maybe that's it. Maybe he has other things on his mind and

our observations just don't take precedence?" Diana spoke decisively. "We may never know. Let's just continue our investigation, and if we turn up anything really relevant, we'll tell Tom. For now, we'll just snoop around on our own."

They all nodded in agreement.

"So, what else is new?" Diana asked, too keyed up to read.

"What do you mean, 'what else is new'?" Beverly sounded confused.

"Well, we seem to have become preoccupied with Haman and his mysterious message and haven't kept up with our own gossip," Diana said.

"She's right," Margie said. "I'm about to launch an amazing anti-Medicare prescription-drug campaign for SOAP to counter AARP's position."

"Right on," Diana cheered.

"Will we see you on the talk shows?" Beverly asked.

"Perhaps, but first I'll definitely need some face work. There's no way I'm going on TV with these wrinkles and indentations."

Allen returned to the sports page, nodding and smirking.

Beverly ignored him. "I think you're right," she said. "The more gorgeous you look, the better you represent your aging constituency. What're you going to have done?"

"I'm researching my options now, but I have to make my decision by the end of next week."

"You mean the day the train blows?" Diana asked.

"I thought we're leaving that topic for the moment and refraining from discussing this on the train?" Beverly said forcefully.

"Well, we're leaving all topics for now because the train is pulling into the station," Allen said, sounding relieved.

The gang bundled up, stood and waited for the doors to open. Allen and Margie left first and Diana and Beverly followed. Halfway down the platform, heading for the stairs, Beverly stopped, gave a mild shriek and turned around.

"What's wrong?" Diana asked, frightened.

"I forgot to put my blazer back on. I left it on the train. It's an Armani!" Beverly said with rising panic. "I wouldn't care, except it's an Armani. You know, an Armani." She kept repeating the phrase apologetically.

"Let's go get it," Diana said, joining her friend to head back to the train.

"No, no, I don't want to hold you up," Beverly insisted. "I can get it."

"No way," Diana persisted. "I'm coming with you."

They walked briskly back down the platform, not knowing when the train would leave again or when the doors would close.

Unsure which car they had sat in this morning, they were about to continue to the front of the train to talk with the conductor when Beverly stopped short. Diana barreled into her.

"What the…?" Diana shouted at Beverly.

"Shh, look," Beverly whispered.

The two women peered into the car. Haman, all alone, was standing in the center of the aisle deep in thought. He was just staring at the ceiling of the train.

* * *

Diana and Beverly stood frozen, staring at Haman. Finally, Diana entered the car.

"What're you doing?" Beverly whispered.

"Just follow and take my lead," Diana whispered back.

"Hi, you also left something behind?" Diana asked Haman.

Haman, startled by the unexpected appearance of the two women, snapped out of his contemplative mood and glared at them.

Beverly walked to the overhead rack and, with a sigh of relief, retrieved her blazer.

Haman watched her, then suddenly seemed to realize what Diana had asked him. "Yeah, I thought I dropped my cell phone, but it ain't here," he said in a thick New York accent.

Diana's first thought was that he sounded very "Brooklyn." He had a deep, sharp voice, which seemed contrary to his very thin, lanky appearance.

"Did you leave it in the ceiling?" she blurted before she could help herself.

"Whata ya talkin' about?" Haman asked.

"Oh, nothing, you just seemed to be staring at the ceiling, that's all. We probably just caught you deep in thought about something. Sorry about that, you know, startling you." Diana tried to cover up her blunder.

"Yeah, I got a lot on my mind at work. I was just pissed about losing my cell phone and what dat would mean." Haman started to look through his backpack. "Ah, it's here, it fell ta da bottom," he said, pulling it out to show them. With a big smirk on his face, he abruptly returned it to his backpack, turned and left the train.

Beverly and Diana watched as he made a quick retreat. Sighing, they both sat down in their usual seats.

"I can't believe I said that," Diana stammered. "I really blew it."

"You're not known for keeping your thoughts to yourself. No surprise there!" Beverly said.

"Yeah, you're right. Now what? Do you think he suspects that we suspect him?"

"I doubt it. We're just strangers to him. I wonder what he was looking at? Do you think that's where he intends to plant the bomb? In the ceiling?" Beverly speculated.

"Actually, yes I do. I think we caught him scoping out the place."

"Do we tell Tom?" Beverly asked.

"Let's see if we can have a brief after-work powwow at Alfredo's to mull over next steps. By then, I should have some information about the shish kebob vendor."

"Let's meet at Sam's Deli instead of Alfredo's," Beverly suggested. "Ron's coming down with a cold and I promised to bring him some chicken soup with matzo balls."

"Okay, I'll email Allen and Margie from school," Diana said. "Let's get out of here before we get trapped and end up in the train yard." They stood up and headed out the train, this time dragging their feet as if they had the whole world on their shoulders.

CHAPTER 12

THE NEW MATH: CRIMINOLOGY 101 PLUS THE ONE-FOUR

Diana left Grand Central Station and stood in the cold trying to decide the best way to get to the police station. Snow was accumulating at a rapid rate and the wind was swirling it around, creating poor visibility. The snow covered the streets but instead of having that magical white, wintry feeling, it had already turned black and gritty by city traffic. Diana observed that the traffic was moving, although very slowly, so she decided to take the bus. She was a true believer in public transportation but preferred daylight to tunnels, so the bus won over the subway most days. Now she walked over to Third Avenue and stood waiting in the protective bus shelter for the uptown bus. She didn't have a long wait. Within minutes, the bus pulled up and she boarded, sliding her Metro card through the reader. There were no seats, so she held onto the strap as the bus moved slowly uptown. It wasn't the most comfortable ride, but it was warm.

* * *

Considering the inclement weather, Diana made good time and arrived at Fifty-fourth Street in only twenty minutes. She walked with care the short half-block to the One-Four, avoiding slipping and sliding on the snowy sidewalk.

Contrary to television shows depicting New York City police stations as dark and dingy places, this one was a new, state-of-the-art, brightly lit precinct building. Diana approached the front desk, which was protected by a bullet-proof Plexiglas shield, shaking the snow from her coat. "Hi, is Lieutenant Venedri in this morning?" she asked, not recognizing the policeman on duty.

"Yeah, are you expected?" he asked gruffly.

"No, but could you tell him his favorite criminologist is here to see him?" she said with a smile.

The humorless officer looked at her as if she were a loony toon, "Are you kidding? What's your name, lady?"

"Professor Diana," she stated, looking quite dejected.

The officer picked up the phone, dialed an extension, and spoke: "Some lady claiming to be a super criminologist is... Sorry, sir, yes sir, I will, sir." He glared at Diana and said, "Go in. I assume you know the way."

"Yes, thank you very much, officer," Diana said gleefully, proceeding through a set of doors leading to the lieutenant's office. Generally, Diana had had wonderful relationships with the police, but occasionally she ran into cops with attitude. She lived for moments like these when they were put in their place.

She knocked on Joe's door and heard him say, "Enter, you troublesome woman!"

Diana went in to find Joe, a man in his late forties with black hair and graying temples, olive skin, and a broad, friendly smile waiting with his hand out to greet her. She shook his hand and gave it an extra squeeze.

"I haven't seen you in a while. This must be a new semester, and you obviously need something from me," he said in a lighthearted tone as he returned to his seat behind a meticulously neat desk. This was a man who was very orderly and organized. Diana always enjoyed the lectures he gave her class because of his wonderful analytical presentations. He made police work sound like a true science, which would account for his outstanding reputation in law enforcement.

"You have my number, Joe. You also know I don't pull any punches." She sat down in front of his desk. "I need to discuss two things with you. First, we've known each other a long time, true?"

"True," Joe agreed. "But before you start your spiel, would you like a cup of our horrendous coffee to warm up? You look like you could use it?"

"Actually, I've had the coffee here, and it's not all that bad. So, yes, I would love a cup. I have to admit, it's freezing outside and I'm not getting any younger."

"Great, I could use one too." Joe picked up the phone and dialed. "Sarge, I hate to bother you," he said, "but I have a special lady in my office who needs to be defrosted. Would you please bring in two cups of coffee so I can keep her company. Yeah, mine black." He looked up at Diana.

"Milk and sweetener, artificial, if possible," Diana responded. She decided to get more comfortable and opened her coat, removed her gloves and hat, then sat back in the chair. Clearly, she was going to be at the station a while.

It only took a few minutes before there was a knock on the door and in walked the Sarge. Diana gasped when she saw him. "My, my, Larry Tasker, you got promoted! Congratulations. So that's why you offered me the coffee. Larry, I'm so proud of you. I guess my tutoring helped you pass the sergeant's exam? Why didn't you tell me sooner?"

"Slow down, Doc. He just got the results this morning, so

your visit was karma." Joe said, defending him.

"Yeah, Doc, when you get to school, there'll be a message on your voicemail," Sarge said. "I swear."

"Wow, you worked so hard to pass. I know you struggled the first time. I'm so glad I could be of help. The lieutenant has such faith in your abilities."

"Don't build him up too much," Joe said, teasing. "I'll never get another cup of coffee again."

"Not to worry Lieu, I've always got your back," said Sarge. He turned and left the office, closing the door behind him.

"We owe you for this one, Doc," Joe said. "He's going to make a great sergeant. He just freezes when he sees an exam."

"Then I guess my visit here was fortuitous," Diana said, taking a gulp of coffee, then pausing before she continued. "I've never asked you to do anything unusual for me, true?"

"Well, some of the lectures you've asked me to give your class may fall into the 'strange' category. But, aside from that, your requests have been on the up-and-up. You have my attention, so get to the point, my dear professor."

"I need to ask a favor, and I need you to just do it without asking any questions yet. Just go with my instincts, please."

"Spit it out."

Diana pulled the photo of Haman from her bag and handed it to Joe. "If possible, I need to find out who this guy is and if he's associated with any shady people."

Joe glanced at the photo. "Give me something more, Doc."

"Okay, he's just someone from the train, he calls himself Haman, but I'm not convinced that's his real name, and I just have a feeling..."

"Say no more, let me see what I can find out. No guarantees. Now, onto Number Two." Joe likely assumed that Haman had been annoying or even stalking Diana and she just didn't want to accuse him yet.

"I want to take a fresh look at homicides. I thought I could get my students involved in a current case. Try to understand the police process first. We would never get to see it in court—too long a timeline. The semester would be over."

"What do you have in mind?" Joe's interest was piqued.

"Well, to tell you the truth, the murder that happened yesterday. You know, the shish kebob vendor. I eat at a restaurant across from where he sells, so I guess I have an interest in finding out why he was targeted. Just a thought." Diana tried to sound nonchalant and arbitrary.

Diana thought she saw a look of shock on Joe's face when she mentioned the vendor. But he recovered quickly and said, "That's an ongoing investigation. You know I can't discuss any details about it with you…"

"I knew you would say that. But isn't there anything on the public record that I could see? You know, the stuff you share with the reporters?" she pressed.

"Well, it's not really my case…" Joe continued.

"Of course it is. It occurred in your precinct. Joe, what's going on?" Diana's sixth sense was on high alert. This was no random killing, she was now sure.

"Look, the case was taken over by a special unit, that's all I can tell you. His name was Charles Bat, he lived in Brooklyn, has three children, sold shish kebobs by day and drove a cab at night. That's all we found out before the case left my precinct."

"Was he an American? What community in Brooklyn did he live in? Did he have a strong religious affiliation?" Diana pressed on.

"Calm down. Yes, he was an American, and I have no idea about his religious affiliation."

"Well, where did his family want the body sent after you were done with it?" Diana wasn't giving up.

"The coroner has that information, not me. I can't help you. Pick an easier case."

"What makes this case difficult?" Diana ignored Joe's insistence to drop it. She was giving this the full-court press. She sensed she had an opportunity to get more information from him. After all, he owed her.

"Ask the Feds," Joe blurted out, sounding quite annoyed. "And that information I gave you is just between you and me. I shouldn't have told you anything, but you can be very persistent and a hard-ass."

"The Feds? Really?" She had been leaning forward in her chair as she threw her questions at Joe, but now she just leaned back quietly, contemplating out loud.

"Joe, thanks," she said. "I know I put you in a difficult position. I really got carried away, but even though I never bought a shish kebob from Mr. Bat, I did notice him on the corner. Death is not something to take lightly. Sorry about my aggressive reaction. Could you go through some easier cases and let me know which one you would recommend?" She tried to keep up the course-curriculum charade, then glanced at her watch. "Gee, I wish I could stay and chat some more, but I've got to get to class. This weather will slow me down."

She rose from her seat and headed for the door, "Thanks again, Joe. You've been a doll, as usual—but you still owe me." Then she bolted out of the office. She didn't want Joe to see how unnerved she was by his slip of the tongue. The gang had really stumbled onto something; but how were Haman and the shish kebob vendor connected?

She left the precinct deep in thought. Joe had gone out on a limb and told her about the Feds involvement in the shish kebob vendor case. Diana decided that Joe was definitely her ace in the hole!

CHAPTER 13

JUST ANOTHER EMAIL?

By the time Diana arrived on campus, she had calmed down. It was a busy day: three classes, office hours, and papers to grade. She needed to focus and focus she did. The snowstorm had not kept her students away, and her classes were packed as usual. After class, she grabbed a quick sandwich in the student union and headed for her office. To her surprise, three students were already waiting to see her. Luckily, they were the only three who showed up, so before long she was finally able to settle down in the quiet of her office.

As she was organizing her desk, trying to find the mound of papers to grade, she suddenly realized that, because it was not geared for the dinner crowd, Sam's Deli closed early, so the gang would have to time their meeting carefully. Diana emailed the gang to discuss the scheduling dilemma. She herself had no difficulty making the early train, but she was not sure about the others. The snow had ceased around noon, which gave street-plowing work crews plenty of time to get the city back on track. She checked the Metro-North "app" and ascertained that there were no train delays; if all worked out and the Westport roads were plowed, they could meet by 5 p.m. This would give them an hour to recap the events of the day and decide on next steps. Diana already knew what she wanted to do, but she needed support from the rest of the gang. Tonight would be an important meeting, and every minute counted.

She had time to grade some papers, which gave her a nice reprieve from dwelling on Haman and the shish kebob vendor. This had been a fun assignment: She had asked the class to select a television show and relate it to one of Robert Merton's sociological theories of deviance. She was reading a terrific paper on how the Sopranos used innovation to achieve the American societal goal of accumulating wealth! Here was an example of wanting to achieve an appropriate goal by using an inappropriate means. "This student is right on," Diana thought. "An obvious selection, but it's a well-written paper." As she was noting her comments on the paper, she heard her computer signal, "You've got mail." She put the paper aside and checked to see who it was from, hoping it was Beverly confirming that she could meet her on the train and give her a ride to Sam's. But when she opened her mail, she saw that it wasn't from anyone she knew. This wasn't unusual; her students emailed her all the time and she was unfamiliar with most of their email addresses. This one was from righteous@letitbe.com. "That sounds like a cute email address," she thought as she opened it.

Diana read the email, then stared at the screen, unsure what to do next. After the shock of the message subsided and she was able to calm down and think clearly, she hit the print button, told the computer to save the message as new and signed off.

Just then her phone rang. She was already frazzled, and the sound made her jump in her seat and started her heart pounding. Slowly, she picked up the receiver and paused, afraid to say anything. Her phone at the school didn't have caller ID. She finally heard a voice from the other end say, "Hello, hello! Diana are you there?"

Recognizing Beverly's voice, she let out a sigh of relief. "What's wrong?" Beverly asked.

"Your call came just as I finished reading a very upsetting email and I was afraid to answer the phone."

"What kind of email? I'm not used to hearing you sound so upset." Beverly said, concerned.

"I don't want to talk about it now. I need to calm down. I feel like I've spent my entire day calming down." Diana could hardly breathe.

"As you would say to me, inhale and exhale, before you have a coronary," Beverly recommended.

"I intend to after we hang up—inhale and exhale that is, not have a coronary. Will you be on the 3:36 so I can unburden myself and get your feedback?

"Unfortunately, no. That's why I called. I actually have to leave work now. My sister needs help on a project, and I told her I would leave early to give her some advice. Not a big deal, but she defers to me on some decorating ideas and needs to tell the contractor her decision by the end of business today. But I'll definitely pick you up at the station, don't fret about a ride."

"Okay, I'll just have to cope. I emailed Allen and Margie, but I haven't heard from them yet. I'll give them a call. See you later. And thanks for the lift. Bye!" Diana was glad to be getting off the phone.

"Bye, stay calm," Beverly responded in a worried tone.

Diana sighed and leaned back in her chair. She stared at her computer for quite some time before getting the nerve to sign on again. Two new emails were waiting for her and thankfully, they were from Allen and Margie. Each had left work early, concerned that the storm would not subside, and they were already home. They reassured her they would be at Sam's by 5 p.m. Diana would be solo on the train, but she decided that was a good thing. She would refine her plan before arriving at the deli.

CHAPTER 14

YET ANOTHER POWWOW A LA CHICKEN SOUP

Diana was anxious to arrive at the Westport train station. It was always nice to arrive home early, but every time she made an earlier train, she ended up with a bunch of high school kids making all sorts of disturbing noises and carrying on the most inane conversations. Who cared that Beyoncé cut her hair and lost some weight? And really, how hot was Justin Timberlake? Needless to say, Diana didn't leave the train with any interesting gossip, just a headache and no additional thoughts about the gang's intriguing situation.

Beverly was waiting for her, so she didn't have to stand shivering in the cold; instead she got into a nice, warm car. "Thanks for meeting me," she said, glad to have such a good friend. "This has not been a very good day. I really appreciate the ride. Josh is attending a meeting in New Haven and I'm not sure when he'll get home."

"Not a problem," Beverly said, still very concerned about her earlier phone conversation with her friend. "Do you want to tell me about the email, or are you just going to continue looking scared to death?"

"I'm okay now. It was those annoying high school kids with their frivolous conversations that I was forced to listen to all the way home. I should have remembered to pack my iPod to drown them out. We'll add my email to our agenda this evening. Let's wait until we're all together. I don't want to deal with it more than I have to." Clearly, Diana was still upset.

"Okay, I can wait five more minutes," Beverly reassured her, knowing her friend well enough not to push. Diana would talk when she was ready. They continued to drive in silence.

Beverly drove north on Route 1 until she arrived at one of the many strip malls along the road. She turned left into the parking area. This mall housed a variety of stores, including a CVS Pharmacy, sport shop, hair salon, fabric store, cleaners and, of course, Sam's Deli.

Sam's Deli had been a Westport staple for decades; it was a daytime hangout where residents met for breakfast, lunch, or just a cup of coffee. As you walked through its doors, the mixture of smells hit you like a tidal wave of foods. Pickles, cold cuts, knishes, cakes, cookies, and bagels were all displayed in the cramped space. In addition, there were numerous displays of all sorts of chips, crackers, and packaged foods. Past the counter and all the displays of food was a small eating area with about twenty Formica-topped tables and faux-leather chairs. The walls were covered with photos of patrons, both famous and faithful.

Allen and Margie had already arrived. Upon seeing Beverly and Diana enter, Allen waved, summoning Harriet, the waitress. She had four bowls of steaming hot chicken soup on a tray. Each bowl contained one large and delicious matzo ball.

"You're a genius, Allen. Just what the doctor ordered," Beverly said with praise. She removed her coat but left on her Armani blazer.

Diana and Beverly joined the other two at the table, and all four lifted their spoons and began to slurp down the soup.

"You'd think we never saw food before," Margie managed to say between slurps.

"This is the perfect day for soup," Allen said. And this soup, it's medicinal."

"Are you sick?" Diana asked.

"No, but I could be if the weather stays this cold and snowy," he said defensively.

Diana needed to get the gang to focus, so she quickly changed the subject. "We have a short window," she said, "so we need to review the events of the day, come to some conclusions, and develop next steps. Beverly, tell them about your blazer."

"Really, Diana. Why are we wasting time discussing Beverly's blazer when we have other issues? Yes, it's lovely, it appears to be Armani, and if there's a sale, we can discuss that on the train," Margie said in a snappy tone.

"Funny lady, her blazer is extremely relevant. She left it on the train this morning, and the two of us went to retrieve it…," Diana started to describe the morning escapade when Beverly loudly began to clear her throat. They all turned to stare at her.

"I just wanted to get your attention," she said. "First, I think Diana has something else she wanted to discuss with us."

"In due time. We should stick with the timeline," Diana said.

Beverly looked at Diana, who gave her a reassuring nod. "Well then, this is my blazer and my story. May I continue?" she asked with a smile on her face. Beverly apparently loved her role as detective and was not going to let her nosy friend take any more of the credit for their morning adventure, especially since she had her own. The gang gave her their undivided attention, and Beverly continued where Diana had left off: "We dashed back to the train to get my blazer. I just didn't want to lose an Armani...,"

"We figured that part out," Allen said.

Beverly glared at him. "Anyway, as I was saying, I really like this blazer, so Diana joined me in trying to retrieve it. We weren't sure which car we'd been in, but that problem was solved. You'll never guess what we saw?"

Diana remained quiet, not wanting to interrupt Beverly's dissertation and risk another reprimand, but Allen and Margie were losing their patience. They both said simultaneously, "Well, what?!"

"Haman. Yes, Haman was standing in the middle of the car just staring at the ceiling. And then you'll never believe what Diana did. She actually walked right into the train and talked to him. Can you believe that we actually made verbal contact with him?" Her voice was full of excitement.

"No way!" Margie exclaimed.

"She talked to him,—what did she say?" Allen asked. He was visualizing Haman staring up at the ceiling.

"Was she ever the smooth character. She told me to follow her lead. I didn't know what to expect. But she was as cool as a cucumber."

"May I complete the tale?" Diana asked. She was dying to relate her own adventure without Beverly's stereotypical imagery. Beverly was doing a pretty good job describing her brazen move, but it was *her* story now. The blazer was inconsequential.

"I guess so," Beverly said shrinking back.

"Anyway, I just asked him if he had lost something, too. He was a bit confused by my inquiry, but when he saw Beverly retrieve her cherished Armani blazer, he suddenly said, yes, he had misplaced his cellphone and thought he'd left it on the train. Well, it was obvious to us that he was fabricating his story."

"At that point, I really blew it," Diana confessed.

"Oh my, what happened?" Margie asked with some alarm.

"She did what she always does," Beverly said, picking up on the story again. Diana was happy to let Beverly describe her blunder. "She spoke without thinking," her friend told the group. "She actually asked him if he lost it in the ceiling!"

Allen and Margie stared at Beverly, then Diana, and burst out laughing. The laugh was infectious, and soon Beverly and Diana couldn't hold it in either; they were all laughing and nodding. Yes, Diana is incapable of not saying what's on her mind.

"How did Haman react to that question?" Allen finally asked after catching his breath.

"He seemed confused!" Beverly stated between giggles.

"Well, I would be too," Margie said.

"I covered my tracks, I think," Diana said.

"She actually did a fairly good job of hiding her blunder," Beverly agreed, reassuring everyone. "I think Haman fell for it hook, line, and sinker and didn't suspect us of suspecting him."

Sometimes Diana could not believe the clichés that came out of Beverly's mouth.

"What does his voice sound like?" Margie asked.

"He's not a Connecticut native, that's for sure," Diana said.

"Definitely Brooklyn," Beverly asserted, presenting herself like a professional linguist.

"What do you think he was doing?" Allen asked, finally getting to the point.

"We both think he was scouting the place and planning where to plant the bomb," Beverly said.

"Aren't you sort of jumping the gun? We really don't know if there *is* a bomb." Margie sounded unsure and frightened.

"She's right," Allen said, "This may just be a coincidence."

At this point, Diana felt it was time to tell her tale of the email. "I need your full attention," she said. "I know we seem to be having fun meeting, eating, playing detectives, and hoping in our hearts that all of the bits of information have no relationship to some terrorist plot, but I think we have to take this more seriously. I have to share an email that I received today while I was at school. Let me read it to you." Diana went into her large bag and started rummaging through it. She finally found the email and pulled it out. She cleared her throat and read: "You nosy bitch. Get out of my business. Tell your friends to back off. We know who you are and we will hurt you. Had any shish kebobs lately?"

Beverly, Allen, and Margie sat in silence as Diana finished reading the email. No one knew what to say. Diana's initial visceral reaction to the email returned. Her hands shook, her voice quivered. She was pale and scared.

"Wow," Allen finally said. "What was the email address?"

"Righteous@letitbe.com," Diana said. "Not an address I'd ever seen before. I would have remembered that one. It's unique. I don't think it belongs to one of my students. And if it is from Haman, how in the world did he know who I am and my email address? How would he get my email? This just doesn't make any sense."

"We really have to think objectively about this," Margie was deep in thought.

"Out with it Margie," said Diana. "You have an idea, what is it?"

"This may sound really silly…" Margie continued.

"Right now, nothing is silly," Beverly prodded. "Spill!"

"Okay, well, remember how Diana asked me to record the fact that Tom seemed unaware of Haman on the train and how he was a disgruntled employee?" she asked.

They all nodded yes.

"Well, Tom knows who we are and that we suspect a plot to blow up the train. What if the email came from him, trying to dissuade us from snooping?"

The gang quietly weighed Margie's theory.

"Margie and I seem to be on the same page," Diana spoke up. "I was thinking the same thing. Let's go with that thought for a minute. What would be his reason for trying to stop us and scare us instead of just telling us to back off?"

"Maybe he didn't think we *would* back off," Beverly surmised.

"You don't think Tom has…," Diana was thinking out loud but was afraid to finish the sentence.

"Say it. Has what?" Allen was at full attention.

"Plans to blow up the train himself?" Diana found the nerve to say it.

"No, absolutely not." Beverly, Allen. and Margie all started talking at once, shaking their heads.

"We really don't know Tom that well," Diana persisted. "I don't think we should eliminate him as a suspect. For all we know, he may be in cahoots with Haman."

"Well, what do you think we should do?" Allen asked. "All our clues point to Haman.".

"I think we pursue this on two fronts," Diana declared.

"Okay, how and what do we do next?" Margie asked.

"Before we decide our next move, I want to report on my visit with Joe at the One-Four. I was so shook up over the email, I forgot to tell you about it." Diana attempted to organize her thoughts. "Margie, please continue to take notes. We need to document this meeting."

"I will," Margie responded, pulling out her pad and starting to write.

"Tell us about Joe," Beverly said. She was getting anxious.

"I gave him the photo of Haman, and he will run a check on him for me," Diana reported.

"Did you tell him why?" Allen asked.

"No, I just asked as a favor. You know, trust my instincts, ask questions later, type of dialogue. But the interesting news," she continued with excitement in her voice, "is about the shish kebob vendor. Only the catch here is, none of you, and I mean *none of you*, can mention this to anyone. I almost feel like we should become blood brothers."

"and sisters," Margie said.

"Again with the humor," Diana said, breaking into a smile, "Seriously, this information came out accidentally in my conversation with Joe, and he made me swear to keep it to myself. Since we're in this together, I feel like I have to share it with you. But silence is golden on this tidbit. Swear?"

All three raised their right hands and said, "Swear!"

"Very well. The murder took place in Joe's precinct, but the Feds took the case away from him!"

"The Feds!" they all screamed at once.

"Shush," Diana pleaded. "This case is not a run-of-the-mill, random murder. I believe that he was a target, and I think he's somehow mixed up with Haman. That's why we have to keep our investigation going on two fronts. Agree?"

Again, the three nodded in agreement.

"So what next?" Allen asked.

"Funny you should be the one to ask," Diana said with a big smile. "Tomorrow, you're going to take me to the mosque!"

CHAPTER 15

MOSQUE MADNESS

Diana and Allen had agreed to meet in his office at eleven in the morning. Services in the mosque didn't begin until noon. They were hopeful that the imam would let them attend the prayer service.

The train ride into the city that morning had been uneventful except for one glaring omission. Tom was absent again. Diana began to pump Mike, the other conductor.

"Mike, you seem to be doing double duty. Where's your comrade?" she teased.

"He said he had a doctor's appointment so he took the day off," Mike replied.

"He seems to get a lot of days off?"

"Yeah, come to think of it, he does," Mike said.

"How long have you known Tom?" Beverly asked.

"Oh, a couple of years, I guess."

"How long have you been working for Metro-North?" Margie asked.

"Twelve years."

"Wow, I thought Tom worked for the railroad a really long time," Diana said.

"Yeah, so what's the point?" Mike asked suspiciously, not sure why he was being bombarded by all these questions.

"Only I would have thought you two would have known each other longer, that's all," Diana said, trying to appear calm and casual.

"Good point, yeah, you'd think. He just sort of appeared, I guess. He got so much time off, we all assumed he was a long-term veteran of the railroad. He probably came off another line. I'll have to ask him about it one of these days. Take care." Mike gave the gang one of his infectious smiles and continued down the aisle, checking passenger tickets.

"Write that down, Margie," Diana instructed. "Your notes are going to become really important."

Margie scribbled down the information from Mike. The gang remained very quiet during the rest of the train ride. Haman was not seated in their car this morning, so they all turned to their respective reading materials, afraid to discuss anything of a sensitive nature while in a public arena, especially the train.

Later, the gang congregated in the center of Grand Central to say their farewells. They had decided to meet at Sam's Deli on Saturday morning to recap the mosque escapade. Diana confirmed that she would meet Allen in his office as they all went their separate ways.

* * *

Diana refused to check any of her emails this morning for fear of finding another upsetting note. Instead she poured herself into her work until it was time to head for Allen's office. She had completed some preliminary research on Islam and felt she was dressed appropriately: long, black skirt, dark stockings, and a cream-colored turtleneck sweater. Everything she'd read about the dress code stated that only the hands and faces of women should be exposed in public. She brought along a scarf to put on her head as a *hijab*, the traditional Muslim head covering for women. She also discovered that the noon prayer on Fridays is called the *juma* prayer and that women may attend. She felt confident she would not embarrass herself and was rather excited about attending the service. Now that she had done her homework, she had a genuine interest in learning more about Islam. "I might even include it in next semester's syllabus," she thought as she read through her notes.

Diana left the Graybar Building and walked briskly toward Forty-fourth Street. As she spotted Allen's office building, her heart started pounding and she felt an adrenalin rush. Her life was never dull, but it had never been this dangerously exciting, either. She entered the building and signed in, as required. She went to the seventh floor to find Allen.

* * *

Allen was sitting behind his desk with a blank stare on his face, almost in a daze. He was not looking forward to visiting the mosque. "What if Haman was there? Then what were they supposed to do? And, if he wasn't there, were they supposed to keep up the charade and attend prayer services five times a day until they saw him? These women, what trouble were they going to get him into?" he worried.

Just as he was thinking how much he was dreading this adventure, Diana peeked her head into the office, followed by her coyote coat.

"Hi, what's wrong?" she asked, noticing the worried expression on his face.

"I'm just concerned about what you want to do, that's all."

"All we're going to do is some old-fashioned legwork," she said soothingly. " Gather some facts."

"What if he's not there?" Allen asked.

"First, let's see if we can even get in. Don't jump the gun. The imam might not permit outsiders. Especially at the *juma* prayer."

Allen stared at her. "What are you talking about?"

"It's just the special Friday prayer, that's all. Come on. At least, just introduce me to the imam," she pleaded. Let's play it by ear. Okay?"

"Okay," Allen said reluctantly. Let's go before I lose my nerve. Take off your coat and leave it here with your purse. I'll lock up."

Diana peeled off her coat and took the scarf she would wear on her head out of her purse. The two of them left the office. Allen led her down the hall to another office.

"Why are we going here? I thought the mosque was on the sixth floor?" she asked, puzzled.

"It is, but the imam works here," Allen said, pointing to the sign on the door that read Omar and Omar, Esqs. Attorneys at Law.

"You've got to be kidding. The imam is a lawyer?" she asked suspiciously.

"Yes," Allen said emphatically. He turned the knob, opened the door and the two of them walked in. The reception area had the look of a lucrative law practice: lovely original artwork depicting beautiful New York scenes on the wall, a plush leather couch with two matching chairs, and a mahogany coffee table. Vases of freshly cut flowers were on the coffee table and the reception desk.

"May I help you?" asked the receptionist, a young woman in her twenties with long black hair, dark eyes, and lovely full lips. She wore a conservative orange sweater and had perfectly manicured nails.

"I'm in the office down the hall and have seen your boss

several times in the elevator. I was wondering, if he isn't too busy, whether he might be able to spare us a few minutes," Allen asked in his confident voice.

"Let me check. His eleven o'clock canceled so he may be able to see you." She dialed his extension and whispered into the phone. Then she looked up with a smile and asked them to follow her.

Allen and Diana were led into a large, beautifully appointed office that captured the essence of a successful attorney. The walls were lined with legal books; the desk was an oversized mahogany partners desk; the chairs were made of very soft and elegant maroon leather; and on the floors were two of the most luscious oriental rugs. To Diana's surprise, the man who greeted them didn't look a day over thirty five. He was about six feet tall, with dark eyes, perfectly coifed black hair, and a warm smile. He wore a custom-tailored, pinstriped black suit with what one would describe as a power tie. She hoped she hid her surprise as he stood to greet them.

"Of course, I know you," he said warmly. "Mr. Diamonds!"

"Yes, you always call me that. But, in reality, I am Allen Stils, and this is a good friend of mine, Diana Jeffries."

"It's a pleasure. I'm Mohamed Omar, but my friends call me Mo."

"Well, I guess you can call us Manny and Mac," Diana joked.

"I actually get that," Mo said with a laugh. "I hope this is a pleasure meeting, not a legal one."

"It is a bit unusual," Diana began.

"Please be seated and tell me," he said pleasantly.

"I teach sociology at Hunter College, and I'm rethinking my current syllabus. I'm a bit disconcerted about the stereotypes that are permeating our society concerning Muslims, Islam, and terrorism," Diana explained professorially.

"Yes, I agree. How can I help you?"

"I want to learn more. I'm a firm believer in not only traditional research but also in fieldwork, which means experiencing realities. For example, I take my students to court to observe trials firsthand to supplement their book learning. I would like to experience Islam by attending a mosque service. Reading about it just doesn't do it for me." Diana hoped her explanation was convincing.

"Ah, I see. Well, you're in luck. I'm from Toledo."

"Toledo?" Allen and Diana asked in unison.

"Which Toledo?" Allen asked, mentally studying the world map.

"You both look very confused," Mo responded. "Toledo, Ohio, of course. "Let me explain. I am part of a progressive Muslim movement attempting to bring the teachings of the Koran into the twenty-first century, especially in the United States. Toledo has one of the few "sister-friendly" mosques, which permit women to worship alongside men. It's still a bit segregated, but at least the women aren't in a cramped hallway or basement."

"You know, for some reason I just assumed that, because this is the United States, the practice of Islam would be more liberal— men and women worshipping together," Diana said as if thinking aloud. "I just assumed our culture would have trumped some of your more 'dated' traditions. Was I ever wrong."

"Culture has a big part to play," Mo replied. "In the most sacred mosques in Mecca and Medina, men and women have always worshipped together. It's definitely a cultural interpretation that has segregated men and women for so long. Anyway, I'm trying to change it. Since I really do come from Toledo, and my mother and father worshipped together in our mosque, I decided to start a similar mosque here in New York. So, I rented the office space downstairs, since it is neither a bathhouse or a camel pen…"

"I don't mean to sound rude," Diana interrupted. "but, yes, I know there are bathhouses around—but camel pens in New York, I don't think so."

Mo grinned, holding back a laugh. "You're so serious, Diana. The rules state that the earth is a mosque except for bathhouses and camel pens, so we can pray almost anywhere."

Although Allen remained relatively quiet, both he and Diana were feeling very relaxed with Mo. He had an easygoing manner and seemed very confident and sure of himself in a nice way. Allen's anxiety was quickly dissipating.

"Could Allen and I observe the *juma* prayer today?" Diana asked hopefully, then elaborated: "I came prepared. I dressed appropriately, brought a scarf to cover my head, and I am way over fifty, so we can forget the *ghusl*."

"You *do* come prepared. Allen, the *ghusl* is a ritual cleansing that is required at certain times. Since Diana has clearly stated she is not of childbearing age, she does not need to perform the *ghusl*. Now for the rules: I really don't want this to be disruptive. You can observe from the back. I would not expect you to actually participate in the *rakas*…"

"Okay, Diana did her research. I'm here for moral support, so please, Mo, fill me in—what's a *raka*?" Allen was feeling a bit squeamish, and his tone was perplexed.

"Let's start at the beginning. The prayers that are required five times a day are called *Salah*, and they are made of up various *rakas*, or positions, such as standing, bowing from the waist, sitting, etc. I think just observing would be best; trying to participate would be almost impossible since you know nothing about our prayers or *rakas*. Diana, you'll be on one side of the room, separated by a low divider, and Allen, you'll be on the other. Okay?"

"Got it, thanks," Allen said. Although he agreed, he did not really want to attend. Now that Diana would be separated from him, he would be the one responsible for trying to find Haman. This was not a chore he wanted.

"Then let's go," Mo said, rising from his chair, "Follow me. Oh, there's one more thing: You'll have to remove your shoes."

"I was prepared for that," Diana bragged.

"I hope I don't have any holes in my socks," Allen said, thinking that this rule only added to his stress; and what if he had smelly feet?

The three of them left the office and headed for the elevator.

"I tried taking the stairs once and discovered that the sixth floor was a no-entrance door—it was locked. So I have to take the elevator. What a bother."

"Do you pray five times a day?" Diana asked.

"I try, but if I'm with a client or in court, I just can't. So I say a few mental prayers. I'm sure Allah (peace be on him) understands."

They entered the elevator for the trip down one story. When they exited, Mo took the lead and headed down the hall toward his mosque. The hall was fairly crowded with men and women milling around, waiting for Mo to unlock the door. Diana noticed that even though the women were permitted to pray with the men, they tended to gather on one side of the corridor, while the men stood on the other. Diana wrapped the scarf around her head and eyed the congregants, searching for Haman.

"I'll leave you two now," Mo said as he started toward the door, keys in hand. "Remember, just stand in the back and observe. I hope to see you after the service." He greeted the worshippers as he walked by them.

"Allen, can you handle this?" Diana asked.

"Now you ask? It's a bit late for your concern. Yeah, I'll be fine," he said in a resigned tone. "Let's go in."

They followed the crowd and entered a huge room that had a wall-to-wall thick, beige carpet, bare walls, and no furniture. Wooden cubicles lined the walls to the left and right of the doorway. The worshippers removed their shoes and placed them in a cubicle. A movable divider about three-feet high separated the room. The women automatically veered left to their side, and the men went right. The area designated for the men was twice the size of the area set aside for the women. Diana surmised that the women were still reluctant to pray with the men. It would take time to equalize, she thought.

Diana tried to stay as close to the divider as possible, hoping to spot Haman and help Allen out with his surveillance.

Once the worshippers were in position, the prayers started. It appeared to her almost like a ballet; each worshipper knew exactly when to perform the *rakas*, and everyone was synchronized. Diana and Allen were mesmerized by the prayers as well as the movements that went with them.

After a while, Mo, who had been leading the prayers, welcomed everyone and began a sermon. The *juma* was unique, Diana knew from her research, because it was the only prayer session during the week accompanied by a sermon.

"Brothers, sisters, welcome," he began. "Today we join together in prayer to reaffirm our commitment to Allah (peace be on him). The topic I wish to discuss today is how we may all live together in peace…"

Diana and Allen strained to hear him, so they just stared into the crowd, trying to memorize as many of the faces as they could.

Once the prayers were over, the worshippers started to depart, many stopping to thank Mo. It was obvious that he was well respected and liked by everyone. This was not surprising; he had a warmth and sincerity that permeated his personality. Diana wondered what had drawn him to the law; he just didn't seem cutthroat enough.

She and Allen lingered to thank Mo. They carried their shoes as they walked out with him.

As Allen shook Mo's hand for a final goodbye, Diana suddenly tugged at her friend's elbow and exclaimed in a loud whisper, "Look!"

CHAPTER 16

LEND ME AN EAR!

Allen reacted quickly to Diana's urgent command and turned just as Haman entered the office next door. Diana, still holding onto his arm, led him quickly back into the mosque.

Mo was flabbergasted by their behavior but didn't try to stop them. He just followed them back inside.

They quickly walked to the rear of the mosque, which shared a common wall with the other office.

"Let's try to hear what's going on," Diana whispered to Allen, pressing her ear to the wall. Allen mimicked her, and they both stood silently against the wall, listening intently.

"What's going on?" Mo asked, interrupting their eavesdropping.

"Mo, it's really complicated," Diana said, ignoring his question. "Do you know who is in that office?"

"I've never seen anyone go in or out of there until you brought it to my attention just now," he answered.

"I know we owe you an explanation, but it may sound slightly bizarre."

Allen stared at Diana as she spoke, not quite sure what she was about to say and how many details she was prepared to share.

"Try me," Mo demanded.

"I had a strange encounter with the guy that just went into the office next door."

"What kind of encounter?"

"Allen and I ride the train into the city, and we always sit with two other women. Anyway, we were saying our goodbyes in Grand Central, when this guy comes dashing out of the tunnel and runs me over. I fell on top of my friend Beverly, and he never even stopped to see if we were hurt. So, needless to say, we kept our eyes out for him on the train, and lo and behold, the next day he was in our car. He actually boards with us in Westport. Then we saw him across the street from our favorite restaurant, and now here. He just seems to be everywhere. I guess we're just curious about someone who is so blatantly rude!"

"So what do you think you will discover by listening at my wall?" Mo asked, no doubt thinking that Diana was some sort of a paranoid nut.

"If we could just listen a bit, maybe it would become apparent," Diana said, placing her ear back to the wall. Allen and now Mo joined her in this endeavor.

From the other side of the wall, they heard a very loud chorus of "Phew, phew, phew!"

"What do you think," Diana asked.

"Sounds like sneezing. Maybe it's a doctor's office," Mo guessed.

"So are we to assume that our mysterious stranger is also ill?

Perhaps that's why he's so rude," Diana said sarcastically.

"Never mind, we've taken up too much of Mo's time as is," Allen said. He was taking control and eager to get out of there as soon as possible. "Thanks so much again for letting us observe your *juma* service. Let's go, Diana."

* * *

"How awkward was that?!" Diana said. She and Allen were seated in his office, feeling like kids whose hands had been caught in the cookie jar.

"Do you think Mo bought my story?" Diana asked.

"What's to buy? You basically told him the truth. You just sounded like a wacko. And as for me, I looked foolish."

"How did you look foolish?" she asked.

"By associating with you, the wacko! I knew something like this would happen."

"What, what would happen? Look on the bright side, we found out where Haman goes on the sixth floor. And, it looks like Tom was right. Haman was probably just visiting his doctor."

"Sure, but I probably alienated a neighbor who's a lawyer!" Allen grumbled, "And I wouldn't be surprised if he told other tenants what a weirdo I am."

"He won't do that. Besides, he's a really nice guy. Perhaps someday we can tell him the entire truth." Diana preferred to look at the situation positively.

Still, behind her optimistic demeanor, she had a nagging feeling. All of a sudden she jumped out of her chair. "Humor me one more time," she pleaded with Allen.

"Now what?" he said, getting up and following her out of the office. "Where are we going?"

"To the sixth floor—I want to check something out," she explained with mounting excitement.

Allen was out of control. "No. No, enough is enough," he protested. "I'm done playing detective!"

"Oh, Allen, we've come this far. This will just take a minute, I promise."

Allen shrugged his shoulders. Reluctantly, he let her lead him back toward the elevator.

* * *

Diana and Allen walked quickly down the hall and stopped in front of the office that Haman had entered earlier.

"What do you plan to do?" he whispered.

"Just have a look. See, the door doesn't have a plaque on it with the name of the tenant like the others do," she whispered, pointing.

"Perhaps the tenants moved in recently."

"Maybe, but I would have put up a temporary sign. You know, made of paper to identify myself until the official building plaque arrived."

Before he could stop her, she turned the doorknob. Allen looked shocked, but relieved when the door wouldn't open. It was locked.

"Now explain that," she demanded as she leaned her ear to the door to try and hear if anyone was there.

"You're nuts! Let's get out of here before we get caught. You're running out of explanations!" Allen pleaded.

"Okay, okay, but I did hear some murmuring…" Diana said as Allen decisively dragged her by her arm toward the elevator.

CHAPTER 17

A BAGEL WITH A SCHMEAR

It was Saturday morning, and the gang seemed to converge on Sam's all at the same time. Their four cars pulled into the parking lot one after the other, grabbing adjacent parking spaces. It almost looked like a synchronized swim.

Ignitions were turned off, doors opened, and the gang marched toward Sam's.

"I need another cup of coffee," Beverly said, moaning.

"Bad night?" Margie asked.

"Lot's of company, and I did a ton of cooking, which resulted in a ton of cleanup."

"Didn't Ron help?" Diana asked.

"He thinks he did," Beverly remarked with a laugh.

They entered Sam's, and Allen led them to "his table." They had purposely met early, before the rest of Allen's Saturday friends joined them.

Allen waved to Harriet, the waitress. "A round of coffee,

please," he requested.

"Thanks," Beverly sighed.

"It appears you two survived the mosque," Margie said.

"Actually, it was a hair-raising event," Allen informed them.

"Now wait a minute, I think it went very well. We should start our own detective agency," Diana joked.

"Stop with the jokes, as you would say to me, and get into the meat," Margie ordered.

Just then, Harriet came over with their coffee and asked, "Anything else for you folks?"

"Four plain bagels with a schmear," Allen ordered.

"Wait, I want my schmear to contain lox," Diana said.

"I want mine with the onions," Margie chimed in.

"I want mine with the garlic," Beverly requested.

"I'm so glad I ordered," Allen said.

"You had good intentions," Margie comforted him. She rifled through her purse to find her pad and paper to start note-taking.

"Out with it! Now you have piqued our interest," Beverly begged.

"Well, first, the imam, named Mo, is quite a gentleman. We had no problem accessing the mosque. It was quite a wonderful prayer session, mesmerizing. I think I really am going to incorporate a section on terrorism and stereotypes..."

"Get back on point," Margie interrupted.

"Oh, yeah, anyway, women are permitted into the mosque, because as Mo explains it, he's from Toledo," Allen said, picking up on the story.

"Toledo, Spain?" Margie, the world traveler, was confused.

"You know, I thought the same thing…"Allen started to say.

"Ohio," Diana said, ending the suspense.

"What does Toledo, Ohio, have to do with a mosque in New York City?" Beverly asked.

"It's a very liberal, twenty-first century mosque that permits women to pray alongside men, that's all," Diana explained. "Mo just wanted to start one along the same lines as the one in Toledo where he was raised."

"Anyway, we were admitted on the condition that we would stand in the rear of the room and just observe quietly. Which we did," Allen continued.

"Well, that doesn't sound very eventful. Was Haman there?" Beverly asked.

"Actually, no…" Diana began.

"So get to the hair-raising part and leave out the rest." Margie was dying to know what had actually happened.

"Well, as we were leaving the mosque, I noticed Haman enter the office next door," Diana said.

"And?" Beverly quizzed.

"And, your wacko friend dragged me back into the mosque to listen through the wall," Allen said.

"No!" Beverly and Margie said in unison.

"And what did you hear?" Margie asked.

"At that point we hit a glitch," Diana said slowly. She looked guilty.

"Oh, no, what happened?" Margie asked.

"Mo followed us back into the mosque and wanted to know what we were up to," Allen explained.

"I told him the truth…" Diana said.

"No way! How could you?!" Beverly screamed. "We still aren't sure of all of our facts. We have more delving to do."

"Delving? You mean snooping," Allen corrected her.

"I gave him only the bare facts—nothing about the plot to blow up the train, the shish kebob vendor, or the threatening email. Just how he knocked us over and keeps appearing."

"Did he buy it?" Margie asked.

"He's an attorney and appears to be very smart. I really don't know. But I do know that when we do figure this out, we'll tell him the whole truth. I liked the guy," Diana said emphatically.

"So, did you ever get to listen through the wall? Did you actually hear anything?" Beverly asked with excitement.

"Actually we did. We heard Phew, phew, phew," Allen divulged.

"Sneezing?" Margie asked.

"Appears so," answered Diana. "Except for one strange thing…"

"Well, what?" Beverly asked.

"If you'd let me finish, you would find out."

"She dragged me back to the sixth floor after we left Mo and she turned the doorknob of the office and tried to listen through the door," Allen stated, still agitated from the experience.

"You're leaving out an important fact," Diana said. There was no sign on the door identifying the tenant. All the other doors had signs. And I heard murmurings behind the door as Allen was pulling me away."

"He was pulling?" Beverly asked.

"I was a nervous wreck. I just wanted to get out of there

before we were caught 'delving,'" Allen said.

"Snooping," Beverly corrected

"Let's get back to the fact that the door had no identification on it. What's the significance of that?" Margie asked while writing feverishly.

"I don't believe it was a doctor's office." Diana stated conclusively.

CHAPTER 18

THIS CALLS FOR ANOTHER CUP OF COFFEE

"Not a doctor's office? What's with all the sneezing?" Beverly finally asked as Diana's words sunk in.

"Maybe he hangs out with a bunch of sick people," Allen guessed.

"Right!" Margie said, giving Allen "the look."

"I really don't know what we should do next," Beverly said pensively.

"Perhaps it's time to confront Tom again," Margie suggested.

"What do we tell him? Do we mention the email?" Diana asked.

"Yes, because if he did send it, and we don't tell him, he'll know we're hiding something from him," Beverly noted.

"Great point, yes, great point. And if he didn't send it, perhaps just knowing about the email would be helpful to him," Diana said, very excited.

"Now we have to wait until Monday before we see him

again—*if*, in fact, he shows up for work," Allen pointed out.

"We're losing valuable time. We need to talk to him in Grand Central when we disembark the train." Beverly was insistent.

"I want to visit my friend Joe again," Diana said. "It may just be time to give him some more information if Tom isn't helpful. Also, I think we should consider following Haman off the train. We need to know where he goes." She had their strategy all planned out.

"Now that sounds like a plan!" Beverly said enthusiastically.

CHAPTER 19

THE FACTS, NOTHING BUT THE FACTS

Diana felt apprehensive as she boarded the Monday morning train. Allen, Beverly, and Margie followed her to their usual seats just as on any other commuter day, but today, she knew, would be a turning point in their investigation. If Tom was onboard, they really had to check in with him. Then she planned to head for the One-Four and, if necessary, she would tell it all to Joe. She needed to know the truth; the timeline they had put together meant that Friday would be the day of reckoning. Time was not on their side; they needed an ally now!

Allen appeared rather relaxed as he accepted the sports page from Beverly. Margie pulled out her mystery of the moment, and Beverly perused the *New York Times* editorials. But Diana just sat there, pondering her next move. She was so deep in thought that she jumped when she heard Tom say, "Good morning, gang!"

"Tom!" she shouted much too loudly, "I'm so glad to see you."

Realizing that Diana was about to "lose it," Margie interjected in a loud whisper, "We need to speak to you when we disembark the train. Where can we meet? It's really important," she stressed.

"Sorry I've been so elusive," Tom said. "I realize you're all upset. I have some news to report as well. I'll wait for you just outside the tunnel. I have a room we can talk in."

They nodded, and Tom continued to collect tickets.

"Thanks Margie. I'm a bit uptight today. I may be wrong, but I really think we're on the verge of discovering something. Quite frankly, I'm scared," Diana confessed.

"Let's be realistic," Allen began, looking up from his newspaper. "This could be a horrible plot that we're about to help abort—or it could just be a bunch of coincidences. I vote for coincidences."

"Really?" Diana responded. "It just doesn't seem possible, all those coincidences. I realize it's difficult to think the worst of anybody, but in this day and age…"

They sat in silence, each remembering their own visions of 9/11, trying to weigh their optimism about the human soul with the evil they knew could permeate it when they heard Tom announce that they were entering Grand Central Station.

Tom was waiting for them as they walked up the ramp and entered the terminal. He motioned for them to follow him, and they walked down a corridor to a door marked Employees Only. He opened the door and signaled them to walk in as he held it for them. The door led to another corridor, and finally Tom led them to Room 101A. Again, he held open the door, and this time they walked into a room that had a small metal table with six chairs around it. They each took a seat and waited for Tom to speak.

"First, I just wanted to say that I took your concerns very seriously, even though you might have thought that I was just humoring you. I ran the photo of Haman you gave me through all of the databases, and he didn't appear in any of them," Tom lied.

"Well, you're probably correct," Allen said. "Diana and I went to the mosque to do some snooping, as you requested…"

"Diana went to the mosque? I thought I told just Allen to go?" Tom was clearly annoyed.

"Yes, but I thought that since I received the threatening email, I should be permitted the opportunity to at least do some of the investigating," Diana interjected harshly.

"What email?" Tom asked cautiously.

Diana pulled out a copy of the email she had received and showed it to Tom. He read it and then put it on the table. He stood deep in thought and finally said, "And why am I first seeing this now? I thought I told you to tell me anything, and I meant *anything*, that seemed suspicious. Doesn't this fall into that category?"

"Well, you seem to be gone a lot…" Beverly said indignantly.

There was dead silence as all eyes were on Tom. "I will have to think about this email," he said. "I'm not sure what to do about it without drawing attention to your escapades." He paused. "What else do you have for me?" he finally asked.

"As I was saying, I think you are correct about Haman," Allen continued. "We didn't see him in the mosque, but we saw him go into an office next door. It appears to be a doctor's office, as you first surmised. We heard a lot of 'phews,'".

"Phews, yes. I guess you heard a lot of sneezing. Well, I think that we can conclude that this was just a big misunderstanding," Tom stated conclusively.

"You are absolutely right," Diana agreed, as the other gang members stared at her in disbelief, "We are just too much into our mysteries, trying to live out one of our books. In this instance, life

114

does not imitate art. Sorry we bothered you, Tom. We were just being silly."

"Oh, no, you weren't," Tom said. "It's really important that everyone remains on alert. You don't want to get too docile and impervious to your surroundings. Terrorism is not going away!"

They all nodded.

"I am concerned about the email," he continued. "Perhaps one of your friends who overheard you playing detectives wanted to spice up the intrigue and sent you that note. I am fairly confident nothing suspicious is going on and that we need not worry the authorities about this. In any event, I can keep my eye on this Haman fellow—but I am sure he is harmless."

The gang thanked Tom and apologized for having bothered him. They got up and left the meeting room. Out in the terminal, Margie, Beverly, and even Allen pounced on Diana.

"What was that all about? You don't really believe it was our imaginations, do you?" they asked at once.

"Of course not," Diana said calmly. "Remember, Tom was on our suspect list. I think something is not right with him, and I'm not sure what it is. I don't know if he purposely wants us off this case or if he's involved. I'm going to see what Joe has come up with."

"So, you were just appeasing him, letting him *think* we're off the case, and yet we continue with our investigations, right?" Beverly asked.

"Right. If I find out anything of importance from Joe, can we all meet tonight after work? Let's try something different. Come to my house. I'll tell Josh to make his great soup. Oh, and by the way," Diana added matter-of-factly. "I know who sent us the email." She quickly turned and walked away, leaving her friends gaping in amazement.

CHAPTER 20

TO PHEW OR NOT TO PHEW

Diana felt calmer now that she knew the gang was onto something. Tom was being evasive, and she just knew he was lying.

As Diana was leaving Grand Central, she spotted Tom walking up Lexington Avenue.

"I have some time to spare, let me see where he's going," she thought.

She followed him for two blocks until he stopped near one of the street vendors selling coffee and pastries for the morning crowds. She saw him purchase a coffee and Danish, but then he paused and a started chatting with the vendor. Diana could not approach the vendor without Tom seeing her, so she held back and just observed. They did seem to be engrossed in a conversation, but Tom did not linger: He suddenly turned and headed down the street, stopping at another street vendor who was selling pretzels and soda. Tom greeted the vendor, purchased a pretzel, chatted for a few minutes, and continued walking down the street. Then he turned the corner and stopped at the cart of yet another vendor, purchasing another cup of coffee. He chatted with this vendor as well and then headed back to Grand Central.

Diana made a mental note to tell Margie to add those strange encounters to her list. Tom was either a street-food junkie, had nothing better to do, or there was indeed something strange going on. She would email Margie later.

Not being able to face public transportation, Diana expertly hailed a cab.

* * *

As Diana entered the One-Four, she noticed the same officer from her last visit sitting behind the desk. She wondered if he would remember her.

"It's you again. Let me see if the lieutenant can see Your Majesty," he said sarcastically. He picked up the phone, then nodded to Diana. As she entered Joe's office, she noticed he was on the phone. He looked up, put his hand on the receiver and said, "Grab yourself a cup of coffee. This call will take about five more minutes."

Diana walked toward the kitchen area. Four detectives were huddled together around a desk and all she kept hearing was "phew, phew, phew." She stopped dead in her tracks and conveniently dropped her purse, giving herself time to do some eavesdropping.

"This is quite the organization," one of the detectives was informing the group. "It really was just a nuisance group for a while, but their new leadership is very aggressive. We have been told to keep them under closer surveillance, but every time we get too close, the Feds seem to stop us." The other detectives were listening intently.

On an impulse, Diana stood up and approached the desk. "Uh, uh…" She was speechless for the first time in her life.

"Yes?" one of them asked. "Oh, I recognize you. You're the professor. The Lieu is always talking about you and your class."

"Yes, that's right. Actually I'm here to discuss that with him right now. Just on my way to get some coffee, and I couldn't help overhearing…"

"Professor, we were discussing a very sensitive case. I don't think …"

"Before you chew me out, first hear me out," she said. "I need you to look at a photo and tell me if this guy is a member of Phew. What the hell is Phew, anyway?" she asked as she rifled through her bag for the photo of Haman.

"It stands for People Hating Elitist Wealth, and it's a neo-Marxist organization," one of the detectives replied.

"Wow, not a sneeze after all," Diana said. She pulled Haman's photo out of her bag and passed it around.

"How did you get this picture?" one of the detectives asked.

"My friend took it with her phone," Diana answered. She observed their reactions to the photo.

"Well, is he a Phew member or not?" she pressed.

"Yeah, he's a member, name's Haman. He's a recent recruit. We're not sure how wacko he is yet."

"I think we're going to need to talk with you, Professor. It seems you know more about this organization than you should. Benny, go get the Lieu, he needs to be in on this one."

"Guys, I know nothing about Phew. I thought it was a sneeze. Trust me, I only know Haman. That is, I don't really *know* Haman—he just rides my train, pushed me over, interacted with a dead shish kebob vendor, and meets in an office next to a mosque," Diana blurted out.

"You never cease to amaze me," Joe said from behind Diana, having arrived in time to hear her remarks. "So, the photo you gave me to investigate turns out to be a Phew member. No wonder I had no luck tracing it. The Feds keep that database hidden."

"Take her into the interrogation room," Joe told the detectives. "We need all your Phew facts, lady, and leave nothing out."

"Joe, seriously, I came here today to tell all, anyway. I need a friend. Bad things are about to happen." Diana followed the detectives and Joe into the interrogation room. As she sat down, she felt relieved to be getting this all out in the open, hoping to finally hear the truth.

CHAPTER 21

SOUP A LA PHEW

All four members of the gang had arrived and were seated around Diana's dining-room table, smelling the potato leek soup simmering on the stove. Diana brought in the steaming bowls one at a time, refusing any help. She was driving the gang crazy in anticipation of what she had learned at the One-Four and, of course, her tantalizing comment as she'd left them in Grand Central Station.

As she placed the last bowl in front of her place setting, she sat down and sighed, "Well, dig in, start slurping."

"We can slurp and listen at the same time," Margie assured her.

"Fine, but this may take some time, so please slurp before the soup gets too cold."

They all nodded, picked up their spoons and began eating.

Diana took a spoonful and began, "I know what phew means…"

They all stopped, spoons in midair, and starting yelling, "Tell us! How could you keep us in suspense?! Out with it now!"

Diana could not help but smile as the gang just stared at her. "PHEW is an organization, not a sneeze. I knew that wasn't a doctor's office…"

"Yeah, you said that before. Out with it," Beverly pushed.

"It's a neo-Marxist group, and it stands for People Hating Elitist Wealth. It appears that they were once some benign organization that just hated the growing schism between the really wealthy and the rest of us. But they have since been taken over by new leadership that is turning them into a radical group. The fear is that they will do something violent. Yes, like blowing up a train…"

"Who told you all of this? Are you certain?" Margie stuttered as she asked.

"I was held captive by a task force at the One-Four and my friend Joe. They knew more than us about the organization, but when I told them about the text message Beverly intercepted, and about spotting Haman on the train staring at the ceiling, and of course about the threatening email, and yes, about seeing him enter that weird office…well, they shared with me."

"Do they think there is an impending danger?" Allen asked.

"Well, let me start at the beginning so I don't lose my train of thought. First, I had to tell them everything, but I did so only after they agreed to share. Remember, the Feds took the case away from them so they're sort of working in the dark as well. Anyway, the shish kebob vendor *is* related to Haman…"

"No way, really?" Margie interrupted as Allen and Beverly spit out some soup they had just tasted.

"Will you stop interrupting me? I can't do this when you interfere with my train of thought. A ton of things happened today and I don't want to leave anything out…"

"Sorry," Margie apologized.

"It appears from what the detectives could sort out, that the shish kebob vendor just passed information. He was like a communication center for them but not really involved. He needed the extra money. But, when the Feds found out about his role, they gave him an ultimatum—work for them or get arrested. So he was going to work for them. PHEW somehow found out that he had turned snitch and had him killed."

"Oh, that poor man, with his sick kid and family," Beverly lamented.

"Haman is new to the organization, and no one knows anything about him. Since the task force has no authority on this case, they can't interfere and overtly help us."

"So I assume they can covertly help us?" Allen astutely asked.

"You got it. All I know is that there is a federal undercover agent monitoring the situation and an entire team watching this organization, so I guess you can say they are taking it seriously."

"What are we supposed to do next? What did they think the text meant?" Beverly asked.

"What do you think we are 'supposed' to do? Leave it to the professionals, of course. They were not sure what the text meant, but they are going to do some snooping around just to make sure we don't get blown up."

"That's reassuring," Margie said sarcastically.

"What about Tom? Did you tell them about him?" Allen asked.

"As a matter of fact, I did. I didn't want them to think that we were a vigilante group trying to save the world. They thought he was probably just some lifelong Metro-North employee who really didn't know what to do and wanted to act macho. They sort of dismissed him, but…"

"But what?" Margie asked, seeing that her friend was holding back.

"I truly believe Tom sent that email to me. I think he is more involved than the One-Four guys give him credit. He may be our ally or our enemy, and I'm just not sure which."

"You really think he sent the email?"

"I am certain he did. He wanted us off this case, and he was trying anything. I think he purposely sent us to the mosque to get us off the scent, and we fouled up his plans by spotting Haman at PHEW."

"You seem to be giving him more credit than anyone else. Why?" Allen asked.

"Just call it intuition."

"Call it anything you like, it's still a pretty strong statement," Beverly said.

"Yeah, I know, but trust me on this one," Diana insisted.

"Okay, what next?" Margie asked meekly, afraid of what was coming.

"Next we follow Haman. Who's with me?"

CHAPTER 22

THE SPY GAME—PART II

"I'm ill-equipped!" Margie yelled.

"What do you mean, you're ill-equipped. We're just going to follow him. What 'equipment' do you need?" Diana answered in frustration.

"Why don't we let the professionals handle this?" Margie asked.

"Because I don't believe they can before the train blows up," Diana yelled back.

They were still sitting around Diana's dining-room table. Soup finished or too cold to eat, they digested what Diana had reported to them.

"Let's all calm down," Allen said, attempting to placate his friends. "Margie could be right—we are in over our heads right now."

"Do you really believe anyone is following this Haman guy around? They don't know anything about him. All the One-Four guys can do is snoop a bit, not really put any resources on the case because they are officially off the case!" Diana tried her best to make her position sound pragmatic.

"What about the Feds? We have to assume that the team they talked about at the One-Four is investigating," Beverly said.

"Yeah, remember that key word *assume*—it makes an ass out of you and me?"

"Now you're quoting from *The Odd Couple*?" Beverly asked.

"If it makes sense…," Diana said.

"Stop, all of you!" Margie begged. "This has made us argumentative and irritable. We're never like this with each other. Just inhale and exhale."

They all stopped talking, stared at Margie and did as they were told. A very good yoga solution.

"We really are risking very little by following Haman," Allen pointed out.

"True," Beverly agreed, "especially if we do it in shifts. Then we don't have to waste an entire workday. I have some time I can devote to it tomorrow. Maybe seeing this through is the best thing."

"Yeah, I also have some free time tomorrow," Margie said. "But maybe we should team up, just in case we do stumble onto something and need to get help."

Diana leaned back in her chair, smiling. "I knew you wouldn't let me down," she said. "Let's divide our day and see what happens. Charge your cell phones tonight—we'll need them tomorrow for our surveillance!"

CHAPTER 23

THE BIG DAY

The gang took their usual seats, all ready for their next adventure. None of them had slept well, but they were prepared for a day of good old-fashioned legwork. They had agreed on a schedule to follow Haman. Margie and Beverly would take the first shift, then Diana and Allen would take the next one, alternating throughout the day. They believed two-hour shifts would be the best. They planned to follow Haman onto the train in the evening and trail him to wherever he went.

They thought they had a great plan. But, lo and behold, when they looked around the train, Haman was nowhere to be seen.

"Now what?" Allen asked.

"There's always tomorrow," Diana said hopefully.

CHAPTER 24

THE BIG DAY - AGAIN

It was déjà vu, as they sat in their usual seats ready for a day of detecting. After all of the hype from their meeting at Diana's house, yesterday had been both a disappointment and relief for the gang of four. Clearly, the Feds were on the case, with New York's finest lurking in the background.

"What are we doing?" Diana thought as she sat facing Margie and Allen, who were busy scouring the train for Haman.

"I see him," Allen mouthed. Beverly and Diana both stiffened, but they had learned not to turn and look. Beverly was tempted to take out her phone and pretend to make a call in order to take a peek, but as she reached into her purse, Allen grabbed the newspaper from her and gave her "the eye." She sank back into her seat. She and Margie were first up, but Allen and Diana decided to join them for the first shift so that they could together develop a uniform methodology of surveillance.

"I went to the library last night and looked for a book on how to spy on someone," Diana whispered to the gang.

"*Spying for Dummies?*" Beverly was quick.

"Not much in demand, I would imagine," Margie

commented, taking her seriously.

"I was kidding," Beverly said, "and being sarcastic. Do you really think there is a huge selection on surveillance techniques for the layman?"

"I'm a researcher, always have been," Diana said. "My instincts are to go to the books to learn. What's wrong with that? Anyway, then I began looking for matchbooks."

"Matchbooks?" Allen looked puzzled.

"Yes, don't you remember all of those mail-in courses you could take that advertised on matchbooks? Well, I thought maybe there was a 'become a private detective in six easy lessons,' and we could get their materials, which I'd assume would include information on how to do a proper surveillance. I didn't have any matchbooks so I went onto the Internet and found a great site called *SleuthSchool.com*. They actually put their syllabus online but it's just an outline. Anyway, they have an entire section devoted to surveillance techniques. I'm going to call their eight-hundred number today and see if they can send me information."

"Don't you think it's a bit late for your sudden interest in proper sleuthing techniques?" Beverly interjected. "It would be easier to just watch some old reruns of *Murder, She Wrote* or *Diagnosis Murder*."

"I did that too. But they actually do very little surveillance on those shows—except for sitting in cars drinking coffee and eating doughnuts."

"When exactly did you get enough time to go to the library, google the web, look for matchbooks, and watch all of those reruns?" Beverly quizzed.

"You know the old saying, 'Give a busy person something to do...'" Diana said. "I only watched two shows, not a marathon of reruns, which cut my time considerably. Time is not on our side, so I just wanted us to be prepared. We have no idea what type of surveillance this will be. For instance, will Haman be sedentary, on the go, or a bit of both? Will he walk, take public transportation, or hail a cab? See, I've been thinking a great deal about our predicament."

"Yes you have, and I'm impressed," Margie said sincerely.

"Well, you do make sense— about what Haman will do, not about matchbooks," Beverly conceded. "I guess we just won't know until we try."

"That's for sure," Allen agreed as the train pulled into the station.

They all bundled up and were ready to quickly disembark so they could monitor Haman's departure.

When the doors opened, they flew out onto the platform and all looked left. Diana was the first to notice Haman. She signaled the gang to follow as she weaved in and out of the crowd until she felt that they were at a comfortable distance not to lose sight of him. But when she looked back to see if the gang was with her, they were gone. A wave of panic ran through her body—they had deserted her!!!!

CHAPTER 25

MEDDLING AND PEDALING

Diana was in a panic, but she nevertheless barreled ahead watching Haman as he maneuvered through the crowd. "He's quite good at weaving," she thought as she kept pace with him. As she and Haman approached the end of the tunnel toward the main terminal area, she spotted the gang waiting for her. Each was wearing a wide grin, looking very proud of their accomplishment. Diana was both relieved and pissed off that they had put her through such an ordeal. But in her heart she had known that they would not abandon her.

As she approached them, they all got into lockstep and followed Haman out of the terminal onto Lexington Avenue. They were thankful that he was not a jaywalker and waited at the light for it to turn green. They followed him across Lexington as he headed toward Third Avenue. At the corner of Forty-fourth and Third, he turned left and entered the building on the corner.

"Now what?" Beverly asked.

"Let's go in," Diana ordered. "We might learn something.".

"No, I'll go by myself," Allen insisted. "We'll be less conspicuous. A gang of four, especially *our* gang of four, is a bit much."

Their silence was enough for him. He quickly entered the building.

The three women shivered in the cold as they waited outside.

"Okay, I'll bite," Diana finally said. "How did you beat me through the tunnel? I thought you'd deserted me. I can't tell you how upset I was! That was a terrible thing you did to me. I may never forgive you."

"Cut the theatrics," Beverly said. "We knew you had him in your sight, so we decided to make sure you didn't lose him. We went back into the train and were able to get through the empty cars faster than your weaving through the throngs of commuters. That's all. You're not the only one who has pondered sleuthing!"

Just then Allen came running or, more accurately, walking quite rapidly out of the building.

"You will never believe this, be prepared…," he almost shouted, his face flushed and his hands shaking.

The women stared at him, then they looked past him at the building's entrance. Haman was leaving the building, walking a bicycle to the curb.

It was Diana's worse nightmare: She could handle a bus, subway, or cab—but she had never anticipated a bicycle. He was a messenger! Even if they had access to a bike, none of them was a good enough cyclist to follow a seasoned New York City messenger!!

"He works for Malcolm's Messenger Service, and he is about to make a delivery," Allen informed them. "Any ideas?"

Diana was one step ahead of Allen. Surveying the traffic, her mind was working in overdrive. Suddenly she ran to the curb.

"We'll hail that rickshaw! Hurry up! Please!" She put her hand up and started shouting, "Stop! stop!" The rickshaw slowed down in front of them, and they all piled in.

131

"Follow that bicycle!" Margie ordered. Then she smiled. "That's a line I never thought I'd say."

"For your information, Miss Detective, this is not a rickshaw, this is a pedicab!" Beverly corrected her friend.

"Semantics, my dear. I think of it as a rickshaw!"

"Rickshaw or pedicab, it doesn't matter, he's getting away!" Allen shouted. Haman knew how to handle his bike and could weave and dart through the traffic at great speed. It was impossible for the pedicab to catch up. The driver was huffing and puffing but he did not have the maneuverability in rush-hour traffic to keep pace with a bicycle while lugging four passengers. Three blocks later, Diana yelled, "Stop! Please pull over, and we'll get out here." She paid the driver as the other three stepped out of the cab. Heads down, they found themselves slowly walking toward Chez Jacques.

"Time for another powwow," she said with a moan.

CHAPTER 26

NO WOW IN THE POW

Dragging their feet, hot air swirling out of their mouths, the gang of four dragged themselves over to Chez Jacques, all in a very pensive mood. Margie knocked on the door as the other three huddled around her for warmth. Jacques opened the door, just shook his head and waved them in.

"Another crisis?" he queried, clearly not really wanting to know.

"It shows, huh?" Beverly replied with a question.

"You know what to do, *mes amis*. Take a seat and help yourselves to some coffee. No breakfast today. I am preparing for a huge lunch crowd."

"Oh, Jacques, we're intruding and taking advantage of your hospitality. We'll leave right now. We just seem to gravitate to your restaurant when we're in need of some comfort food. Let's go, gang," Diana said apologetically.

"No, no, please stay. You are such good friends. I did not mean to sound flippant. I insist!"

"Well if you insist," Allen said and led them to their usual table before Jacques changed his mind.

After removing their gloves, hats, scarves, and coats, they marched silently to the coffee urn, each taking a mug, pouring their coffee, and finally sitting down at their table. The silence was deafening as they began to slurp their hot coffee and slowly warm up. Suddenly Henri appeared with a tray of croissants, butter, and jam— the ultimate continental breakfast. Jacques just could not leave them cold and hungry. After all, he spent his life feeding people. How could he leave his four dejected-looking friends with just a cup of coffee?

They smiled at Henri and thanked him for their morning sustenance. His presence broke their silence.

"Now what?" Margie finally asked.

"We need a recap," Diana suggested.

"What's to recap? We tried to follow Haman to determine what he was up to regarding blowing up our train, and we were unprepared. We never anticipated that he would be traveling around Manhattan on a bicycle, since the numerous times we've seen him, he's been on foot or on our train. Is that enough of a recap?" Beverly sounded exasperated.

"Aren't you the testy one?" accused Allen.

"Well, we're nowhere near knowing what this guy's up to, and it's Wednesday! Our window is rather small, don't you think?" Beverly responded.

"Obviously," retorted Diana

"Breathe, everyone. We need to calm down and decide how to link up with him again," Margie said.

"I can't," Diana whispered.

"What?" Beverly asked, "did you just say you can't? Why not? You've been the biggest snoop of all! What's your problem?"

"I was only going to observe for a while, remember? I have a class to teach. Let me think this through and we can do a chat room later today. Maybe you guys can think of something. I'm running out of steam." Diana finished her coffee and croissant, looked at her watch and stood up.

"You've gotta be kidding?" Margie almost screamed. "How can you desert us now? We've all been in this together?"

"I'm not deserting you, but I can't skip class. It's early. I'll think of something. I have to go."

Allen, Beverly, and Margie stared at her as she put on all of her outerwear.

"I swear, I'll think of something, just not now," Diana said, and she walked out of the restaurant.

CHAPTER 27

A LITTLE LEG WORK

Once Diana left the restaurant, her pace picked up. In fact, she definitely had pep to her step. She retraced the gang's footsteps and ended up in front of the building on Forty-fourth and Third Avenue.

"What a sneak I am," she thought as she walked into the building," but we need action, and I need to get to class." Malcolm's Messenger Service was just off the lobby. She did not knock on the door, just opened it and walked right in. The office was small with room for a counter and some storage behind the counter for packages. On the far left of the room was a bike stand that contained some bikes that were not yet in use. A young woman with long curly hair and heavily painted lips greeted her.

"May I help you?" she asked politely, after she gave Diana the once over and determined that she might be a potential customer.

"Well, I was hoping you may be of help. I teach at Hunter College, and one of my students is in need of a part-time job to help pay for school. He is a terrific cyclist, and I was wondering if you had any positions available?"

The receptionist's attitude immediately changed. "And he can't talk?" she asked.

Diana was ready for this retort. "Yeah, he can talk, but I had an appointment in this building and happened to notice your office. Gotta problem with that? I guess you don't want to hire dependable smart messengers, huh?"

Just then the phone rang and the receptionist was forced to turn her attention from Diana, allowing her some more time to peruse the premises. She noticed an in-out board. Haman's name did not appear on it. She took out a pad from her commuter bag and began to quickly write down the names of the messengers on the board. She could hear the receptionist arguing with a customer, apparently about a delayed pick-up and delivery. The sign-in board listed the time each messenger signed in for the day and then noted sign-out times and destinations for deliveries. Based on the sign-in times, Diana narrowed the names down to three—Raymond Cherry, Tom DeWitt, and Calvin Hammand.

She needed to ask the receptionist one more question, and then she knew exactly what her next step would be. But just then she spotted a door at the far end of the room with the word "Office" on it. She quickly moved in front of the door and knocked before the receptionist noticed or had time to stop her.

She heard a brusque, "What d'ya want now, Camille?"

Diana quickly opened the door, "Sorry, it's not Camille. I just had a quick question, and Camille is on the phone with a customer," Diana said in her sweetest voice.

Again, she was given the once over, and after being quickly sized up as a potential client, the boss asked her to come in and have a seat. Diana was not in a schmooze mood and just stood in front of his desk, put her hand out and introduced herself. The boss stood up and accepted her hand as Diana said, "I am on the faculty of Hunter

College and need some information about your messengers. Do you have flexible hours?"

The boss introduced himself as Malcolm, the ultimate messenger. Diana stifled a laugh, "Yes, I have heard wonderful things about your messenger service. That's why I want one of my students to work for you. Now, about those flex hours…"

"Doc, may I call you Doc? Please, sit, sit. I want to tell you all about how Malcolm's Messenger Service came into existence. Such a story, you won't believe it."

Before she could stop the words from leaving her lips, Diana blurted, "Is there a short version?"

Malcolm looked at her with such a hurt expression that Diana was forced to backpedal. "That didn't sound right," she admitted to him. "It's just that I have to get to class and I'm strapped for time. I would love to hear about how Malcolm's became the ultimate messenger service, but I do need to hurry."

"Yes, of course. Just, please take a seat, and I promise not to waste too much of your time."

Diana reluctantly sat down, knowing she had sealed her fate; she was now his captive audience.

"Well, I come from a small town in Indiana. I think as soon as I could walk I wanted to dance…"

"Dance…and how is that related to biking?"

"If you're in such a rush, you can just leave, lady," Malcolm reprimanded her. Diana quickly realized that she had better keep quiet or she would never get out of there with the information she needed. She sat back in her chair, virtually giving up. Malcolm continued, "I was a closet dancer, dancing to every sound I heard. Moving my body in ways it never knew. I had flexibility and grace. I was in the perfect zone when I was dancing. But, I was afraid to tell my parents that I wanted to go to dancing school. So, I saved my allowance, earned extra money doing chores for my parents and babysitting. Indiana is a state known for its bikers, so I naturally was given a bike when I was about four years old. I virtually ignored it. Yeah, I could ride it, but it had no function for me—until one day, when I was fourteen, I saw an ad in the local paper for a new dance school in the next town over. Well, the next town over was fifteen miles away. So after school, I hopped on my bike and pedaled to the next town. I went to the dance school and watched a class. I talked with the owner, and she told me I could start a class, but I had to get to the school by 4:30 each day. That would be quite a hustle for me, but I said I would. So, every day I would bike the fifteen miles each way from school just to dance. Until one day, my Dad caught me riding to dance class. I told him I was secretly training to be a cyclist so he wouldn't think he had a faggot for a son…?

"What?" Diana almost shrieked.

"Well, lady, you wanted the short version, remember? Anyway, the next thing I know, I'm the proud owner of the most expensive racing bike my parents couldn't afford. It appeared I was going to have to give up my pliés for time runs. The rest is history."

"Malcolm, that short version is not good enough. So you got my attention. What happened to your dance career?"

"Take your coat off, stay awhile," he said, eyeing Diana. "I had to give up my lessons because now my Dad was going to manage by cycling career. I had to join the cycling team at school, and quite frankly, I was damned good at it. I actually got a scholarship to Indiana University, and you know what a great cycling team they have. But, college was not for me and I really missed dancing. So I left school and moved to New York City in hopes of returning to dance. But the life of a dancer is a short one, and I got a knee injury that sidelined me. I went back to what I did best. I got a job as a messenger, which put less strain on my knee, and I worked my butt off. The guy I worked for took a liking to me and taught me the business angle of messengering. He was single, no kids, and when he decided to retire to Florida, he sold me the business at a great price. I have tripled revenues and plan on opening another branch in Brooklyn. So, I guess you can call me the dancing cyclist."

"Actually, I don't want to call you anything. But now please, tell me about how you hire your messengers. Do you have flex hours?"

"You certainly are persistent. Are you and this student, you know, getting it…"

"No, you have a filthy mind. Just answer my question, please."

"I try to screen my messengers because you never know what they will be carrying around for our clients. They need to be bonded. That can take time, so sometimes I hire, then bond. If they are not bonded, I make sure they don't go to clients who will give them anything of value—you know, like diamonds. And all of our hours are flex since we have a lot of students, actors, you know the type, working for us. As long as I get the daily coverage I need, I don't care when they work. Camille is a great scheduler, so I leave that up to her."

"So," Diana continued, "If a messenger begins his day at 8:45 a.m., when would he be finished?"

"Anytime. That's what makes flex hours so great. Some days you may work four hours, another day, ten hours. It's quite variable."

"Do you have a minimum number of hours they have to work each day?"

"Yeah, as a matter of fact, they do have to give me at least four continuous hours in a day. Can't have too much flex, ya know. Has that been helpful?"

"Yes and no. Oh, one more question, I know you must share your story with your employees. Is anyone else who works here a dancing cyclist?"

"As a matter of fact, I just hired a kid about a month ago. Looked kind of nerdy and was reluctant to give me references. He finally admitted that he also had the dancing stigma. But, strange, now that you mention it, he sounds like he's from Brooklyn. Coming from New York City, dancing is just not what it is in Indiana. You know," Malcolm continued as if talking to himself, "I better check him out more carefully."

"Would that be Calvin Hammand?" Diana asked, praying she would get away with that question.

"Na, Raymond Cherry. Calvin, or as we call him Cool Cal, is into Harleys," Malcolm answered, then suddenly stared at Diana. "What do you really want, lady? What are you up to, anyway?"

"Nothing, really. I was just reading your in-out board while Camille was on the phone, I have a photographic memory, you know... Thanks for the information and, I am really glad you forced me to listen to your story. It really was interesting. If I know anyone needing a good messenger service, I will definitely recommend them to the dancing cyclist!!!" As she babbled, Diana tried to make her exit.

"But what about your student?!" Malcolm yelled as she fled.

"Oh, I'll pass the information on to him. It's up to him now. Ta, ta!" she answered on her way out. She believed she was now closer to knowing Haman's identity, and she had to admit that the story of the dancing cyclist was a hoot. It was time for her next stop.

CHAPTER 28

THE ONE FOUR AND COUNTING

Diana's head was spinning. She felt that all-too-familiar knot in her stomach, which always occurred when she was overtaken with time-related stress. Add to that the overwhelming guilt she was feeling about deceiving her friends. She decided to walk the few blocks over to the One-Four to help calm herself down before she talked with Joe.

To Diana's relief, the sarcastic officer at the front desk was not there. Instead, a young female officer was manning the desk. "May I help you, ma'am?" she asked.

"How I hate being called ma'am," Diana thought, but she answered in her sweetest voice, dreading a nasty rebuke, "I'm here to see Lieutenant Venedri. He's not expecting me, but if you tell him the lady professor is here, I'm sure he will give you permission to open your pearly gates."

Diana could not seem to keep contempt out of her voice, and the officer responded with a deadly glare. She picked up the phone and dialed Joe's extension. After a few seconds, she spoke. "There is some pain-in-the-neck lady here…,yeah….right…that's what she said…gotcha, okay." She hung up, hit the buzzer, and Diana just walked in without acknowledging her.

Diana was about to knock on Joe's door when he flung it open. "If I didn't like you so much…!"

"Really, Joe! The cops that you put at the front desk are just plain rude."

"I'm not getting good feedback on you, either. People in glass houses…"

"Okay, I will try harder. I was so ecstatic that the usual cop wasn't there that I thought I could actually be nice, but you know me and those words that just keep on coming."

"Unfortunately, I do. Your mouth is like a Duracell battery. Now, tell me why you're here. And, please sit down and unbundle."

"Thanks." Diana opened her coat and removed her hat, scarf, and gloves, then plopped in a chair in front of Joe's desk. "Do you want it in a nutshell?"

"Just start talking."

"Well, I assume you concluded that we would ignore your orders to stay off the Haman case? Correct?"

"Yeah, but one could always hope."

"Good, then we can avoid all of your lectures and I can get to the point. We decided to tail Haman to find out what he was up to…"

"You what? Are you serious? Don't you know that could be dangerous? Didn't we tell you the Feds were on the case? What do I have to say to you to knock some sense into that middle-aged head of yours?"

"I thought we agreed that you wouldn't lecture me."

"You made that up."

"That's beside the point. May I continue now?"

Joe glared and nodded.

"We tried to follow him yesterday, but he wasn't on our train. So, we met again today, and he *was* on the train, but the rickshaw could not keep up with his bicycle in all of the rush-hour traffic…"

"What are you talking about? This isn't Hong Kong? I know you're skipping something."

"Sorry, my mind kind of jumped to fast-forward. We followed Haman to where he works, and it turns out he's a messenger. So when he left his office riding a bicycle, we hailed one of those pedicabs to follow him, but it was impossible. So after a quick powwow breakfast, I left the gang to do some of my own snooping, without their knowledge. They will be pissed off at me, but that's another issue. Anyway, he works for Malcolm's Messenger Service, and there were only three messengers on their in-out board who left at the time Haman arrived to work. None of them had Haman's name, so we can assume Haman is an alias…"

"That I figured out a long time ago," Joe broke in, sounding a bit peeved.

Ignoring Joe's last statement, Diana continued, "I talked with Malcolm. He loves to tell the story of how he became a messenger. He thinks of himself as the dancing cyclist…"

"Relevance?" Joe snapped.

"It happens to be quite relevant, if you would give me a sec to tie the pieces together," Diana snapped back. "He insisted that I stay to hear his story, and he doesn't take no for an answer. I assumed—and this time I was not making an ass out of you and me—that anyone who applies for a job must also sit through his spiel." Diana paused, anticipating another snide remark from Joe, but he just sat there, listening intently. "I asked him if there were any other dancing cyclists who worked for him...?

"Just one minute. Before you continue, could you fill me on what a dancing cyclist is?"

"Aha! You are hooked, as was I," Diana said chuckling, and related Malcolm's story to Joe.

"Interesting, but relevance?"

"Again, give me time to tie it together. He told me that, about a month ago he hired a messenger who also had been stigmatized by an urge to dance. Malcolm confirmed that, in fact, he hired this guy without really doing his usual background check because, as I surmised, he sympathized with his plight..."

"How do you know it was our Haman?"

"Because, as he was telling me this, a lightbulb went off and he realized that the guy sounded like he was from Brooklyn, and since a New York City kid could easily escape the stigma of wanting to dance, perhaps something was awry."

"Awry? Are you writing a novel? What's with awry?" Joe asked mockingly.

"Funny man, then something 'stunk.' Is that a better word choice?"

"Yes. So what else did you discover? So far, I got nothing."

"As I said, there were three names on the in-out board. One name was Calvin Hammand..."

"That was a good assumption..."

"But a wrong one. Somehow I got up the nerve to ask him if Calvin was our guy. Before he actually grasped my question, he answered it and said no, it was Raymond Cherry."

"Evans, Evans, get your ass in here, pronto!" Joe suddenly screamed through the door. Diana jumped in her seat and was amazed at how fast the door flew open. There stood a disheveled, somewhat overweight, middle-aged man with white hair and horn-rimmed glasses..

"Yeah, Lieu, what?" he asked.

"We got a name, finally. Talking to the professor today is like bleeding a stone. Anyway, check out a Raymond Cherry. Could be our Haman. Tell the rest of the task force, see if anyone knows this guy."

"I'm on it," he said, then turned and closed the door as he left.

"Good job, but why didn't you just give me the damn name. The dancing cyclist was an interesting story, but…"

"Spare me. You'd never have taken me seriously unless you knew how I arrived at my conclusion. So don't play games with me."

"You are absolutely correct, and I apologize. Now get out of here so I can get back to work!"

"Trust me, I was just leaving," Diana said smiling. "Oh, and I like you, too!"

CHAPTER 29

FESSING UP AND AWAY

Diana was distracted all day. She conducted her classes by rote because she just wanted time to think and plan next steps. What if Haman was not on the train tomorrow, and Friday was D-Day? How were they going to stop the train from being blown up? Should they just not go in on Friday and save their own skins, or..."

Her phone rang in her faculty office, interrupting her chaotic thoughts.

"Yes," she answered abruptly.

"It's us," Beverly said, a bit startled by her sharp voice.

"Us, what are you talking about?"

"It's all of us," Allen, Beverly, and Margie chimed in. They were conferencing.

"Oh, sorry," Diana said with a moan. "I was deep in thought when the phone rang."

"What's up?" Beverly asked.

"What do you mean, 'what's up'?" Diana asked guiltily.

"You were so weird this morning, and time is getting short.

Have you thought of next steps?" Beverly asked, worried.

"As a matter of fact, I did some next steps on my own. It was on my way to school, so…," Diana sounded very guilty and much too apologetic.

"You left us out of the loop?" Margie asked, hurt.

"I thought we were in this together, planning and snooping," Beverly said, a bit accusingly.

"It's okay by me," Allen added, glad that he had not been dragged into one of her schemes again.

"Don't be pissed. I think I figured out Haman's real name, and I've already given it to Joe. So we are now on the right track. I know that Malcolm's Messenger Service messengers work on flex hours, so we have no clue what days and what hours Haman works. I think we should hope he's on the train tomorrow so we can…"

"You can't be serious?!" Beverly screamed. "We can't attempt to follow him again!"

"No. I know that. But we can follow him to his building. I know that once he starts his shift, he has to work at least four hours. After we see him enter, we can return to his building four hours later and watch for him. Once his shift ends, then we follow him!" Diana finished the thought, very proud of herself. Especially, since she had had no idea what the next step would be until she actually started talking to the gang. "What a great gang," she thought, sitting back and smiling.

"Wow, that's a plan," Beverly said, sounded elated.

"Yes," Margie agreed.

"I guess so," Allen added reluctantly.

"Are we supposed to forgive you for flying solo," Beverly asked.

"Please," Diana begged. "I will give you all the details

tomorrow. Breakfast is on me—but I think we should avoid Chez Jacques before we are banned from there."

"Agreed," they all echoed.

CHAPTER 30

ON THE TRAIL AGAIN

Margie pouted, Beverly stared, and Allen read the sports page while Diana squirmed. The gang was not going to let her off the hook as easily as she had thought—except for Allen who seemed most content when things were *not* happening because his comfort zone was his routines.

"How many times do I have to apologize?! Let it be," Diana begged.

"What are you talking about?" Beverly asked demurely.

"I'm not letting her get off without some sort of rebuke," Margie stated defiantly.

Allen just kept reading in silence. Diana wasn't sure if he was giving her the silent treatment or if he just didn't care.

"If you want me to rationalize, here goes," she told them. "All of you were able to go back to work without having to schlep around town while I just made a few extra stops along my route to work, which I didn't mind doing. So, what seems to be the problem?"

"You could have at least shared your intentions with us while we were eating breakfast," Beverly scolded.

"And given us the option of either participating or deferring to you," Margie continued.

"Or not," Allen added.

"Or not what?" Diana asked.

"I just didn't want you to think I didn't care," Allen said.

Diana glared at him, but Allen just smirked and returned to reading about the Yankees spring-training plans.

"I have another plan," Diana whispered, dreading their reaction.

"And you really think we care," Margie said.

"Yes I do, because it means we can stay warm and cozy all day in our respective offices and accomplish our plan to follow Raymond Cherry alias Haman. So there!"

"Okay, I'll bite," Allen said, lowering his paper and looking at Diana with renewed interest as Margie and Beverly nodded in agreement, reluctantly giving in.

"Allen, you spend your entire life eating out, correct?" Diana asked.

"What are you talking about? Alice is a very good cook!"

"Perhaps a slight exaggeration," she conceded, "but you do eat out quite a bit, so let me finish my thought…"

"Shh," Margie kicked Diana as Tom approached the gang for tickets.

"Morning, Tom," they greeted him in unison. Tom smiled at the gang, nodded and continued down the aisle.

"Thanks, Margie. I think I should purchase some shin guards if I continue to sit with you. My legs are all black and blue."

"Stay on point," Beverly pleaded.

"Right. Well, I promised to treat you all to breakfast this morning and not at Chez Jacques. Allen, is there a diner you frequent that has a young waitress with a really pronounced New York accent?"

"Height, weight, hair color?" he asked, stifling a laugh. Beverly and Margie stared wide-eyed at Diana, perplexed by her request.

"Funny, funny. I have a point to all this—just answer my question."

"Yes," Allen replied with a smile.

"I knew it!" Diana beamed. "*That's* where we will be dining this morning!"

"But," Beverly asked, "Haman aka Raymond Cherry, was on the train this morning and according to our timeline…"

"Shh," Diana interrupted her, "I have that under control. Our timeline is safe. We will have all of our answers this evening, I just feel it!"

"Where?" asked Allen

"Where what?" the three women asked at once.

"Where do you feel it," Allen asked innocently.

"In my left breast," Diana answered matter-of-factly, which shut Allen up.

CHAPTER 31

HATCHING A PLAN OVER EGGS AND BACON

"I miss Jacques,'" Beverly whined as she squeezed into a booth next to Diana.

"You are so spoiled," Allen teased. "This is your basic New York Greek diner. I'll order."

"I know you'll clog my arteries, but who cares, we're not paying," Margie said, salivating over the thought of greasy, gooey food.

"Allen, do you have a favorite waitress?" Diana asked, getting down to business.

"The young one with the heavy New York accent?" Allen reiterated.

"Yes. But before you get her, I need to write something. Give me just one minute, and then go find her and ask if she would do us a really big favor."

"What kind of favor?" Allen asked cautiously.

"Make a phone call," Diana said.

The three of them looked at her bewildered and curious. Somehow, they knew that whatever she had in mind would make sense, but now it most definitely did not. Diana rummaged through her commuter bag, pulled out a pad, grabbed a pen from her purse, and slowly began writing in bold print. The three just watched her until she looked up, nodded to Allen, and said, "It's time. Go get her."

Allen slid out of the booth and approached the counter. He spoke briefly to the waitress standing behind the counter who seemed to recognize him. She nodded and went through the swinging doors into the kitchen. Allen returned to the booth and sat down with a smile.

They waited in silence until a petite young woman with curly red hair, a turned-up nose, and very red lipstick approached them. Her name tag said Susan.

"Hoi, Mista S," she said.

"Perfect!" Diana yelled out before she could stop herself.. They all stared at her. "Sorry, I get excited when everything seems soooo right."

"Gerty said you ast ta see me. What's up?" Susan asked.

"I'm giving a surprise party for my nephew and need to know when he'll be getting off of work tonight without anyone getting suspicious," Diana answered. "The people he works for would recognize our voices, so we thought if a young woman called, no one would think it was strange. I wrote down what you should say to make it easier. Would you help me out?" She asked in her most compelling voice.

Susan thought for a moment, "Yeah, what tha hell, I can do that. Let me see the paypa." Susan perused the script Diana had written and nodded as she read it to herself. Diana pulled her cell phone from her purse, opened it and rummaged through her purse for Malcolm's Messenger Service business card.

"*Voila!*" she said holding it up. "Are you ready, Susan?"

"Yeah, dial, this ain't too hawd."

Beverly and Margie just sat in silence watching and waiting in anticipation, wondering what she would say and what ramifications the answer to the question had for them.

Diana dialed and quickly handed the phone to Susan.

It seemed like an eternity, but finally Susan spoke, "Hoi, duh, moi frient Raymond told me ta meet him afta his shift taday but fo'got to tell me when his shift was ova. Yeah, yeah, tanks a lot."

The gang sat staring at Susan. Finally, Diana blurted out, "Well, what time is his shift ova today?"

"3:30. Is dat all? I need ta get back to woik."

"Yes, just a minute. Allen," Diana requested, "Give Susan something for her help."

Allen rolled his eyes, pulled out his wallet, and handed Susan a ten-dollar bill.

"Gee Mista S, tanks a lot. Let me know if ya eva need any help again." Susan turned and walked back into the kitchen.

"Ova?" Beverly looked at Diana and laughed.

"It just came out. I don't know where it came from. Was her accent perfect or what? Allen, you're a genius! And, I know, I'll put the ten on my tab!"

"Before we continue deciphering your plan, can we now order our greasy breakfast?" Margie pleaded.

Allen looked up and waved over the woman who had been behind the counter. "Four of my usual, Gerty. Thanks."

"Splain, Lucy," Beverly demanded, looking at Diana.

"This was one of my simpler plans, and you'll all appreciate it."

"If you ever get to telling us!" Margie's hunger and

impatience was getting the best of her.

Gerty brought over the coffee and poured a cup for each of them. As soon as she turned and walked away, all eyes were back on Diana.

"Just to reiterate, we discovered yesterday that following Haman is impossible. But I'm not sure we even need to follow him while he's at work. Granted, he may stray during working hours and go places we may need to know about, but I think we need to follow him when he gets *off* work. So, instead of going back to Malcolm's Messenger Service in four hours and waiting out in the freezing cold for him to return, I thought it would be best to get there when his shift is 'ova' and begin our surveillance then!"

"That makes sense," Beverly said, "but why did we have to go to such great lengths to find the young woman with a New York accent?"

"Because when I left Malcolm yesterday, he was a bit suspicious, so I didn't want anyone to think someone was after our Haman. If a young woman who sounded more like him called, no one would suspect anything. I doubted that a bunch of older adults could pretend to be young New Yawkers. And it appears my plan worked!"

"So, what's our next step? I know we all show up at Malcolm's at 3:30 to follow him, but what are the logistics, etc?" Beverly asked enthusiastically.

"First, Allen goes back to Westport on the 3:06 train, which gets him in an hour later. He then goes to Alfredo's."

"I like that—it's a plan," Allen said, smiling, and sat back so Gerty could place plates of greasy eggs and bacon in front of everyone.

"I'm totally confused," Margie admitted.

"As you should be," Diana said with a smirk. "Beverly,

Margie, you meet me at 3:30 in front of the messenger building. And Allen, have your cell phone on, because when you get our call, you'll need to meet us at the train station in your car. Now, dig in so we can get to work. This could be a very long day."

CHAPTER 32

ON THE TRAIL YET AGAIN

Diana stood shivering on the corner of Third Avenue and Forty-fourth Street waiting for her cohorts. She noticed a Ray's Pizzeria with window seats across the street and decided that, once Beverly and Margie arrived, they would keep warm there; and if they must, eat pizza all afternoon.

She felt it was time to tie up some loose ends. She whipped out her cell phone and called the One-Four precinct to get an update from Joe. Unfortunately, she was told he was gone for the day. "I thought for sure he would have some feedback on who Raymond Cherry is and what he's up to," she mused to herself. "Well, I guess we run solo on this one."

"Yoo-hoo, yoo-hoo!" Beverly screamed in her ear.

Diana jumped. "What's the matter with you?! Are you trying to scare me to death?"

"I've been trying to get your attention, and you seem to be in another world," Beverly quipped.

"Sorry about that. I was deep in thought. It takes my mind off of how cold I am. Where's Margie?" Diana asked, looking around.

"How would I know? Oh, there she is, bounding down the street," Beverly said, pointing.

"Bounding? Is she a dog?" Diana laughed.

"Check her out, she's bounding." Beverly said giggling.

"She hates being late even though she's always late, so I guess she's attempting to run." Diana continued to laugh as she eyed her sixty-four-year-old friend, who had never worked out and who led a fairly docile life, attempting to "bound" down the street bow-legged.

"Okay, what's so funny?" Margie demanded as she reached them, huffing and puffing.

"Nothing, let's go warm up with pizza," Diana proposed.

"Sounds good to me," Margie agreed.

The three women crossed the street and entered the pizzeria. Diana immediately grabbed the window seat before anyone could stop her.

"Yay, we have a great view of the front entrance to the building. Haman should be here any minute. Maybe we won't have to order anything," Diana said hopefully.

"Oh, that's not fair. I wanted a slice," Margie said.

"Then go up and get one really fast in case we have to scoot out of here pronto," Diana ordered.

"Okay, okay, calm down. Let me just remove my coat..."

"Stop!" Diana screamed. Everyone in the pizzeria froze and looked at her.

"Not you!" she yelled to the room. "Margie, put your coat on, let's move it! He just entered the building with his bike. It shouldn't take him long to check in and leave again. We have to be ready for our surveillance."

The three women scurried out of the pizzeria and weaved

their way across the street, positioning themselves as inconspicuously as possible.

"Now what?" Beverly whispered.

"Why are you whispering? He's not here yet," Diana scolded. "We'll just follow him. If I were to guess, I would say he'll just head back to Westport, but we should be prepared if he makes any other stops. It's so cold out, we should wrap our faces with our scarves— he'll never recognize us!" The three rearranged their scarves; their faces were now hidden, only their eyes peered through. They looked at each other and started to laugh. No doubt the people on the street thought they were typical New York crazies—except for the fur coats and designer purses.

Finally Diana caught her breath. "Are you thinking what I'm thinking? I feel like one of the Egyptian mummies in an Elizabeth Peters mystery, all wrapped up. Except that we're breathing."

"Right on," Margie agreed, smiling under her scarf. "Except we could be in an Agatha Christie novel as well. She was married to an archeologist…"

"Enough," Diana said.

It was difficult just standing around, since the pedestrian traffic had to walk around them, but they held their ground until Beverly spotted Haman leaving the building.

"There he is," she whispered.

"Stop with the whispering! No one can hear you, let alone him," Diana retorted. "Let's follow him—but we must keep our distance." Haman walked past the women without even a glance in their direction. Their sighs of relief were audible as they began to walk behind him. It appeared that Diana's assumption was correct, and he was heading toward Grand Central Station. But then he kept walking.

CHAPTER 33

WHOEVER SAID BEING A GUMSHOE WAS EASY?

"Just when I thought this would be a cakewalk surveillance, we actually have to follow this guy," Diana mused, gasping as she pep-stepped to keep up with Haman. Beverly and Margie were just behind her.

"He really knows how to weave through the crowds. Where's he going?" Beverly said out loud. At least it wasn't in a whisper.

"I think he's heading back to Allen's building," Diana guessed. "What happens if he enters the building? We can't get in because Allen's not there. I sent him to Westport!"

"Wait, look!" Margie stopped short and pointed. "He's meeting someone in front of Allen's building. Beverly, quick, get out your phone and take a picture."

Beverly started to rummage through her purse and finally pulled out her phone. She opened it, pointed it toward Haman and his cohort and snapped. "Whew, that was close! I was afraid I would miss the shot," she said with relief.

Margie leaned over her shoulder to see if Beverly's photo was clear enough and not another selfie. Both women were so intent on studying the picture they didn't realize that Diana was no longer with them. They looked up to see her standing within hearing distance of Haman and his friend, pretending to be searching for something in her purse. They froze in their spot, afraid to make a move that might cause Haman to notice them.

"Pretend you're talking on the phone, and I'll pretend to be listening as well," Margie instructed. Both held their breaths until Diana turned and rejoined them.

"What just …?" Beverly started to ask.

"Shh, I think he's about to return to Grand Central and the train," Diana said. "I'll tell you all about it then. I need to write it down—my memory is not what it used to be. The over-fifty memory-loss nonsense. Give me a sec…"

"He's walking toward us, you don't have a sec," Beverly said.

"Okay, you two follow him. Let me go into the lobby and write it down before I forget what was said. Don't worry, it'll just take a few minutes. I'll call you when I'm heading toward the station, and you'll tell me what train you're on. Go, just go." Diana pushed them away as she turned and walked toward the building.

Beverly and Margie were petrified that they would botch this up without Diana, but they took deep breaths and walked at a good distance behind Haman. His associate had gone in the other direction, so they didn't have to worry about being noticed by his companion.

Diana was right again, and Haman entered Grand Central. He was in time for the 4:36 train. They had plenty of time, so they followed him into the train and sat down where they could see him. Margie whipped out her phone and called Diana.

"We're on the 4:36 train," she reported. "It's a local, so I hope he gets off at Westport. Where are you?"

"I'm on my way. I was just going to call you. I should make the train with minutes to spare. I'm almost there. Which car are you on," she asked through heavy breathing.

"We're on the second from the back, so just hop on as soon as you get here," Margie said. "We have a seat for you."

"See you in a minute." Diana huffed as she ran for the train. She quickly checked her watch, and it was 4:31 when she entered Grand Central. She ran past the information display and glanced quickly to ascertain the track. "Why didn't I ask which track they were on, what a jerk I am!" she thought. But luckily her train was on the upper level, Track 18, so she hurried toward it and jumped on just as the doors were closing. Since she'd hopped onto the last car, she had to barrel her way to the back of the car. She pushed the heavy doors open and entered the second car. She spotted Margie and Beverly immediately and plopped down next to them. The seats were three across.

"Whew, that was close," Diana said catching her breath. "I should have asked you which track. Still, it worked out fine. Where's our guy? Oh, I see him—he's listening to his iPod, good. He'll zone out and we can talk. This time, my dear friend Beverly, in a whisper!"

Diana needed to calm down after her marathon run to the train. Margie and Beverly were bursting at the seams in anticipation of what she had written down, but they knew their friend well enough. When she was ready she would share.

Finally, Diana leaned down, grabbed her purse and pulled out the pad on which she'd written her notes.

"Their conversation seems somewhat significant," she told the other women, "and I was able to get the gist of what they were saying. Remember, we missed the initial encounter, so I came in the middle of the conversation."

"Stop making excuses and give us what you got," Beverly demanded, just as she'd heard them say on *Law and Order.*

Diana passed them her pad to decipher. Her handwriting was

terrible.

"What does this mean?" Margie asked after she stared at the words for a few minutes.

"Well, to recap," Diana whispered, "Haman said that tomorrow is important, and if it went well, he would get 'promoted.' The other guy said, not necessarily, since this was just his first assignment. Not to get his hopes up, to just do what he's told. The master—strange choice of words, don't you think—is the only one who can 'promote' him. Then the other guy also said, 'Tomorrow is just the beginning, there's so much more that must be done.' At that point, I think they noticed me, and the other guy passed Haman a piece of paper and said to follow the instructions to a tee! That's when I turned around and joined you because it appeared they were done talking."

"Sounds ominous to me," Beverly said.

"I agree. Our premise about blowing up the train tomorrow seems to be on schedule," Margie whispered in a shaky voice.

"Ditto and ditto," Diana said very softly, deep in thought.

"What next?" Beverly asked.

"Give Allen a call and tell him we're in the back of the train and to meet us there with his car. By the way, how's his driving? Do you think he can tail Haman in the dark?"

"Now you think of that? Perhaps I should have been the one sitting in Alfredo's," Beverly remarked.

"And you think you can tail him?" Margie asked.

"Yes I do! I'm quite the daredevil behind the wheel of a car. Haven't I told you about my escapades?" Beverly sounded a bit hurt.

"Another time. For now, we are stuck with Allen. But what escapades are you talking about?" nosy Diana had to ask.

"The time I went wild behind the wheel of the golf cart for

one," Beverly said defiantly.

"That doesn't count," Diana answered with a laugh. "You were drunk, driving both in the cart and with the irons. That was a disaster, you are now and forever permanently banned from that golf course."

Beverly pouted as Margie dialed Allen to tell him when to meet them. Then they sat back and kept their eyes on Haman—just in case he surprised them and disembarked before the Westport stop.

CHAPTER 34

"FOLLOW THAT REFLECTOR!"

As the train neared the station the three women huddled together in the aisle watching Haman. He was standing at the door, ready to exit quickly, and the women were blocked by a line of commuters waiting to disembark.

"Beverly, call Allen! Make sure he's waiting for us," Diana ordered.

"Got it," Beverly said and pulled out her phone, hit speed-dial, and waited for Allen to answer.

"We're pulling in now. Are you there?" Beverly spoke quietly into her phone and nodded to Diana and Margie as she clicked it shut.

The train pulled into the station and stopped, and the doors opened. Haman walked off as the women pushed their way behind him. He ran down the station stairs and turned left, heading for the taxi stand. Diana glanced around, saw Allen's SUV and motioned to the women to follow her. They got into the car as quickly as they could, and Diana instructed Allen to turn around and follow Haman. He stopped at the bike rack, unlocked a bike, put on a helmet and reflector vest, hopped on and started pedaling away.

"Oh, no, not another bike!" Diana said in frustration. "What now? Allen, how slowly can you follow this guy?" she asked

"I'm 73, slow is my middle name."

Haman was exiting the parking lot and now he turned right, heading toward Route 136. He was pedaling faster than they expected so Allen didn't have to crawl behind him. Haman turned left on Route 136 and rode toward Norwalk.

"That reflector vest he's wearing makes following him rather easy. Seems strange that he's so cautious about his biking safety but will probably blow himself up tomorrow," Diana commented.

"We don't know that," Margie said with a quiver in her voice,

"You're right, I didn't mean to scare you, but… Allen, look! He turned into that side street—make a left turn!" Diana yelled.

"I'm not deaf, just old," Allen said as he turned the car into a narrow paved street. The street sign read "Avery Place," but it was a rather desolate road, lined with woods and devoid of homes. As they followed Haman down the street, they noticed a brightly lit building ahead. It appeared to be a warehouse.

"Stop the car," Diana ordered. "Pull over there behind those bushes. I don't want Haman to notice us. He must be heading toward that warehouse—there's nothing else here. If we leave the car, we can walk the rest of the way. The car is totally hidden so anyone coming down this street won't see it. Allen, do you have a flashlight, just in case we need to see something?"

Allen stopped the car as directed, reached into the center compartment and whipped out a flashlight. He smiled proudly at the women—until he tried to turn it on. The batteries were dead.

"So we'll be careful," Diana assured the gang. "But, as we told you Allen, you should be reading more Elizabeth Peters books

You'd be a lot better prepared." Beverly and Margie laughed. because they got the joke. Allen just glared.

They got out of the car and felt the ice-cold wind on their faces, but quietly closed the car doors and started to walk toward the warehouse.

Getting as close as they dared, the gang hid behind a row of dense arborvitae, shivering in the frigid night air and unsure what to do next: wait for Haman to leave the building or try to get a closer look. The gusts of wind intensified the iciness that permeated their bodies. Freezing, they huddled together, teeth chattering, but they were determined not to leave until they had successfully completed their surveillance.

Suddenly, a deep voice whispered from behind: "Turn slowly, do not speak, and walk quickly over to the black van behind those trees."

They turned in unison and stared into the barrel of a Glock 9 mm semi-automatic gun. Too frightened to speak, they obeyed without a word. As they walked toward the van Diana thought, "What have I done now?"

CHAPTER 35

THE TRUTH AND NOTHING BUT THE TRUTH

Beverly, Margie, and Allen just stared at Diana. as they sat in the van. They were all shivering with fear now. Diana was frightened but also upset, not quite sure what to say to her dear friends. After all, it had been her idea to pursue this suspicious set of events, even though the others had seemed to be onboard with her. But, what if something happened to them? No one would know where to look. She ignored their stares, too upset to talk. The van was now in motion, and they just rode silently. It seemed like a lifetime before the van stopped, though in fact, it was only ten minutes. The door slid open.

"Let's move it, now. It's time to talk."

They quickly got out of the van and were led into a red brick building. Diana thought it looked familiar, but they were entering the building from a loading area and in the dark it was difficult to tell exactly where they were.

Once inside, they were led into a conference room. The four were motioned to sit down and left alone.

"Where are we? Why does this look so familiar?" Diana heard herself say out loud.

"So you found your voice?" Margie asked.

"This is my fault entirely. We should've just minded our own business. But the signs on the train kept reminding us 'If you see something, say something!'" Diana said.

"Cut the crap!" Margie blurted and put her hand over her mouth, embarrassed by her sharpness. "Sorry, but we're in this together. You're right, we saw something unusual. Granted, we went a bit overboard in our investigation, but we're all very thorough in everything we do. Why should this be any different? Besides, it's obvious that something is asunder."

"Asunder? This is not some third-rate mystery novel," Diana said. Something is really wrong! Perhaps we'll learn the truth before…"

"Before what?" Beverly asked.

"I'm not sure what will happen to us now," Diana whispered, too scared to say the words.

Just then, the door opened and Diana gasped. "What are *you* doing here?"

In the doorway stood Tom and Joe Venedri, both looking quite upset, in fact ready to explode. Joe's mouth was snapped shut and his lips were pursed tensely. Tom, on the other hand, just looked frustrated. He appeared to want to say something but also knowing that if he did, he might go ballistic, so he just entered the room and sat down. Joe followed but remained standing. Since Diana was the only one who recognized Joe, the others stared intently at Tom. The silence was deafening, until Tom spoke.

"In case you're wondering where you are, you're in the Westport Police Station. They lent me the use of their conference room for this meeting."

"I knew this place looked familiar!" Diana blurted out.

Tom glared at her and continued, "My name is Tom Reynolds, Special Agent Tom Reynolds of the FBI. I've been undercover on the transit system since 9/11. My assignment is to identify potential terrorists and, obviously, thwart any terrorist activities. It appears that the four of you were rather astute in fingering Haman aka Raymond Cherry. I was under strict orders not to let you or," Tom glanced over to Joe, "the New York City Police Department know anything about the nature of this assignment. I'm sure you can appreciate the need for secrecy when dealing with anyone involved in terrorist activities. Our job is to uncover not only the operatives but also the brains behind these operations. It takes time and patience to discover the scope of some of these plots."

"But why...," Diana stuttered.

"For once, all of you, and especially *you*,"—Tom was looking straight at Diana—"are to keep absolutely quiet until I give you permission to talk. You're being told way too much, as is, and I'm just hoping we can trust you. But it was either being forthcoming," Tom continued. "or quieting you in other ways." At this point, a look of panic appeared on all four faces, causing Joe to interrupt.

"Doc, we are just trying to make you understand the magnitude of what's happening and hope that the four of you will respect the need to keep everything you hear tonight under wraps. That means, do not tell your spouses and certainly, after you leave here tonight—and you *will* be leaving here, I assure you—never discuss this even amongst yourselves. Got it?"

The gang all gave a simultaneous sigh of relief and nodded to Joe.

Tom gave Joe an appreciative glance and continued, "I asked Joe to join us, because you uncovered Haman's real name, and he was running it through all of our databases. I couldn't let the New York City Police Department go off on its own investigation and mess up what we had been working on for the last six months. So, in case you all don't know him, this is Lieutenant Joe Venedri from the One-Four precinct. I have included his task force on this investigation, just so we have a coordinated effort in thwarting any attempt on the train.

"As you are aware, PHEW has been on our radar for quite some time, but it has been only recently that they have become a more militant group. Home-grown terrorism is not new to this country. Just think about Timothy McVeigh and Oklahoma City, the bombing at the Atlanta Olympics, and the Unabomber. So, we've had Haman and his organization under surveillance for quite a while now, including intercepting phones calls. And, yes, just to read your minds, we have used warrants to tap their phones. I hate to admit this, but as a result of your amateur sleuthing, we've had all of the Metro-North trains checked out by bomb-sniffing dogs and double-checked for any security breaches. So far, we've turned up nothing to suspect that an explosive will be detonated tomorrow on the train. Our encryption team worked on the message that Beverly wrote down and found nothing to warrant a red flag for tomorrow. This is not to say that we won't have added security on duty tomorrow—we will. But the feeling is that nothing is scheduled for then and not in the near future, either. Our interceptions indicate that PHEW is doing some housecleaning. Getting rid of its passive members and enlisting more militants. We are sure that in the future they will launch some sort of offensive, but not at the present. Now you may speak."

"Tom, is it really safe to go to work tomorrow?" Margie asked.

"As far as we can tell, yes," he responded. "Can I guarantee that nothing will happen? No."

"Are you really pissed at us?" Diana asked.

"Yes, you put me and my team in jeopardy. I tried to get you off the trail by sending you to the mosque, but you ran into Haman, and that put the kibosh on that attempt. I even sent Doc that threatening email to try and scare you off the case, but that backfired too because, I have to admit, you are very clever and it became obvious that you no longer trusted me.

"You have to learn to leave these investigations to the professionals," he reprimanded them.

"Except that we didn't know you were the professional," Diana retorted.

"Point taken, but now you do, so please just deal with your respective lives and leave amateur sleuthing off your to-do list," Tom advised.

"I have to ditto that," Joe added. "Doc, I know you are unabashedly the most curious individual I've ever met, and I'm glad you included me in your sleuthing, but I have to agree with my colleague: Keep out of police business."

"Are we free to go?" Allen asked.

"Not yet," Diana said. "What was that warehouse that Haman went to in Norwalk?"

"Another job he has," Tom explained. "He's a packer for a mail-order business. An online hardware store. Like a Home Depot, but much smaller. His uncle owns it, and when he moved here to stay with him, he said he wanted to work off his rent by working a few evenings a week. It all checked out, trust me."

"Then why were you parked out there doing surveillance?" Diana asked.

"You're sleuthing again," Tom said. "He's under surveillance. We've established that. We're tracking all of his comings and goings. His uncle's business is on the up-and-up. The FBI has this under control. Now you're going to get into the van, and we'll drive you back to Allen's car, and you'll go home to your families. Got it?"

"Got it," Diana agreed.

CHAPTER 36

SOMETHING'S BUGGING ME

The gang climbed into Allen's SUV and buckled themselves in. Allen turned on the ignition, backed the car from behind the bushes and began to retrace his steps back to Westport. Nobody spoke. Finally, Diana decided to break the ice.

"I'm bushed," she said. "This has been a very tiring and trying day. Allen, would you mind dropping me off first?"

"Is that all you have to say?" Margie asked

"Well, we were specifically told not to talk about this, even amongst ourselves, so I suggest we just keep quiet," Diana said.

"I disagree," Beverly said. "I think we have a lot to talk about, and I don't care what they told us."

"Well, not now. Just take me home," Diana persisted.

They drove in silence until Allen turned into Diana's driveway. As soon as he stopped the car, Diana opened her door and signaled them to follow her while she exaggeratedly put her fingers on her lips to indicate they should say nothing. Beverly shrugged but got out; Margie smiled and followed her. Allen reluctantly turned the key and got out of the car.

Once inside her house, Diana invited the gang to take off their coats and head for the dining room, promising to join them there shortly with bowls of Josh's great soup.

Again, they just sat in silence, aware that any attempt to get her to explain now would be fruitless. She had a plan and intended to stick to it.

Once everyone was served soup, Diana finally spoke, "I didn't want to talk in the car…"

"That was blatantly obvious," Beverly said.

"Well, I couldn't very well explain why I wouldn't talk in the car while in the car, could I?" Diana asked.

"Huh?" Allen said as the others just waited for her to explain.

"Because I assume they bugged Allen's car," Diana stated matter-of-factly.

"And why in the world would you assume something so ridiculous?" Beverly asked.

"I can't believe you! What's so ridiculous? Tom's an undercover FBI agent, the warehouse is under surveillance by the FBI, Allen's car was left there while we were being interrogated…"

"We weren't being interrogated," Margie corrected her. "You're just overly dramatic. We were being threatened, scolded, reprimanded, admonished, chewed out, but definitely not interrogated."

"Whatever. Anyway, we were specifically told to butt out and not discuss anything. So, what better way to verify that we listened to instructions than to bug Allen's car?"

"If you had made that statement two weeks ago I would have had you committed, but in all honesty, it may be true," Allen said.

"So now that we know not to talk in Allen's car, let's talk here," Diana continued. "The most critical thing we must decide is whether to go to work on the train tomorrow."

"I'm not terribly brave, and I could work from home tomorrow," Margie said almost in a whisper.

"Me too," Beverly agreed.

"You too, what? You're not brave or you can work from home tomorrow?" Diana asked.

"Both."

"Me too," Allen chimed in.

Diana sat back in her seat looking thoughtful. "I'm going," she said.

"Why? Tom said he couldn't guarantee our safety," Margie said.

"Tom's been on our train for quite some time, and I would guess that on any one day if we asked him whether he could guarantee our safety, he would say no," Diana declared.

"Excellent point," Beverly agreed.

"Perhaps," Margie allowed.

"What the hell!" Allen said, "I'm going too."

"I certainly won't tell you what to do," Diana said, "because if anything does happen…"

"We're all adults, and we'll make up our own minds," Margie asserted. "Whoever shows up tomorrow, that's fine. Whoever doesn't, that's fine too. Let's not discuss this anymore, okay?"

All three nodded in agreement.

"Next point. Margie do you have a copy of that text message with you?" Diana asked.

"Sure, it's with all of my notes. Why?"

"I think we should take another look at it. I don't believe the FBI decoders, or whatever they're called."

Margie went into her bag and pulled out her notes. She handed Diana the page with the message.

Diana glanced down at the paper and read out loud:

"Haman, next Friday RT?

Yes

7:20

As planned

The bridge

Awaiting instructions, be prepared-major blast"

"How in the world could or would anyone assume that this was *not* a plan to blow up a bridge?" Beverly asked.

The three sat looking very pensive. Finally, Diana spoke. "I'll play devil's advocate," she said. "Let's be objective. Here's another interpretation: RT is the other person's name, or nickname, for argument sake. Perhaps they're meeting near a bridge to have some sort of party? We refer to having fun as a blast, right?"

"Poppycock," Beverly interjected. "I think you're grasping at straws. For one thing, the person who texted him had a screen name, so he knew who it was. The RT would not be his name…"

"You didn't write down his screen name." Diana spoke rapidly: "What was it? That could be really important. Perhaps that would help the Feds."

"I really botched up," Beverly said dejectedly. "I didn't even write down Haman's screen name. You're absolutely right: That was a really important clue. I guess that's why we're considered amateur sleuths."

"We'll just have to work with what we got," Diana reassured her friend.

"And what have we got? Nothing. The FBI discounted this text, so let's just go back to being normal commuters reading our mysteries, discussing politics, and eating out!" Allen begged.

"Sounds like a plan," Margie said.

"I guess so," Beverly reluctantly agreed.

There was silence. The three of them looked at Diana, waiting for her to agree as well, but she gave no sign of acquiescing. She sat there deep in thought, and finally said, "We'll see."

CHAPTER 37

NONE BUT THE BRAVE

Diana ran up the stairs to the train platform after slamming the car door. She and Josh had fought over her taking the train today.

"Better safe than sorry," he kept saying.

But she was adamant about taking the train and had agreed to phone him every fifteen minutes while riding into the city.

The cold weather was really slowing her down, and she found herself gasping for breath as she arrived on the platform. She was alone on the spot—no one else was there yet. She wondered if the word was out that the train could blow up today. But as it neared 7:20, the usual throngs of commuters poured onto the platform. Many had learned to remain in the station house until just before the train arrived to prevent frostbite. Margie, Beverly, and Allen appeared just as the train was pulling into the station.

"So they all decided to brave the commute," Diana thought as she pushed her way onto the train to grab their regular seats.

None of them was in a jovial mood this morning; in fact, they all had circles under their eyes from lack of sleep. Diana leaned over to Margie and whispered, "Do you see him?"

Margie glanced up and with a panicky look on her face, then nodded yes. The four of them sat in silence for a few moments. Margie's hands visibly shook, Allen just stared at Haman, and Beverly nervously played with her hair. The tension rose as the train pulled away from the station. Diana whipped out her cell phone and called Josh, "First call," she said. "We just left the station, and all's right with the world." She hung up.

Tom's voice came over the loud speaker. "Ladies and gentlemen, your attention please. As you're all aware, we occasionally hold terrorist-preparedness drills as part of our Homeland Security program. Today, our train has been selected to be a part of this drill, so please don't be alarmed by the added presence of the state troopers, bomb-sniffing dogs, and militia. This is just a drill, so please continue with your reading and napping. Thank you for your cooperation."

"Wow, they *did* take this seriously," Diana said. "Margie, how did Haman react to Tom's announcement?"

"He just listened and smirked," Margie replied.

"Smirked, really?" Diana asked.

"Yeah, he looked cocky," Allen added.

"Do you think that he believes he outsmarted us?" Diana pressed.

"He doesn't know anything about us or our investigation, so why would his smirk be related to us?" Beverly asked.

"Who's sitting next to him?" Diana asked.

"He's in the middle seat. Some business guy is next to him by the window and no one is seated in the aisle seat," Allen said.

"Margie, here's my cell phone. Just hit redial every fifteen minutes and say, 'All's well,' and hang up. It's just Josh, he's a bit nervous, and I promised to call him every fifteen minutes, just do it please?" Diana begged.

"And where will you be?" Beverly asked. "Why can't you call your own husband?"

"Because I'm going to change seats and sit down next to Haman," Diana declared.

"And how will you pull that off without him wondering what's going on since everyone is settled in now?" Margie asked.

"Easy! Allen, you know everyone on this train…who do you recognize?"

Allen glanced around and lo and behold, standing right behind him but not wanting to sit, was Larry, a sometimes commuter buddy.

"Larry!" Allen called out a bit too loudly. "How are you? Come, have a seat, please."

"He's good, really good," Diana thought.

"But you don't…" Larry said.

"Please take my seat, I have to get some sleep, and this group just won't let me rest," Diana reassured him. "I'll take another seat." She rose quickly to change seats before Larry changed his mind.

She walked down the aisle and plopped down next to Haman, pretending not to notice him. She glanced past Haman and out the window, wondering how many bridges the train crossed on its way into the city. Diana defined a bridge as any expanse of tracks that didn't have solid ground under it. Gazing out the window, she quickly lost count—and they were still in Connecticut! As she survived each bridge-crossing, she became more and more agitated, anticipating only the worst. Haman, on the other hand, seemed oblivious to his surroundings, probably because he knew which bridge to blow up.

After the first twenty-something bridges, Diana settled down and pulled out her mystery book of the moment and placed her commuter bag under the seat. She pretended to read as she kept her eyes subtly on Haman. She even managed to turn the pages of her book, but there was no way she could concentrate on reading. First, she was way too tired, and second, she was much too apprehensive. She settled into her phony reading routine as Haman sat motionless beside her with his phone in his lap.

The first member of the terrorist-drill unit marched down the aisle; a soldier with a very large gun strapped to his waist. He had penetrating, deep blue eyes and took a long look at everyone. He appeared to be memorizing their faces. Diana could just hear his supervisor asking him what the woman in the fifth row, outside seat, was wearing and reading. But she did notice him taking a slightly longer look at Haman than the others in her row.

It seemed like a parade of security forces because next came the bomb-sniffing dog, who took his job very seriously. His nose never stopped. Haman must have been clean as a whistle because the dog didn't miss a step as he passed their seats.

Finally, Tom came by to check tickets; he clearly was not pleased to see Diana seated next to Haman. She even thought he would ask her to move, but he just shook his head and kept on checking tickets. Still, she thought, "if looks could kill, am I ever dead."

A state trooper appeared next and decided to remain on their car. He stood behind Allen and the gang at the exit doors. It gave him a good vantage point for spying on Haman.

After the parade of security finished their "exercise," Diana lost interest in pretending to read and started to doze off. But just as they approached the Blue Bridge, which ran over the East River, Haman turned on his phone. Diana perked up, heart pounding. She thought the entire train could hear it: thud, thud, thud.

Haman stared out the window and then, all of sudden, he

began to press buttons. Diana peered over and saw the words:

POW. RT successfully completed

Diana looked around. Nothing happened. The train kept going, Haman just smiled, and Diana almost cried.

CHAPTER 38
LET IT BE OR THE BIGGEST LET DOWN EVER!

As the train pulled into Grand Central Station, Diana stood up, but her knees were weak and wobbly. She was glad that the train was swaying as she attempted to walk down the aisle toward the gang. No one took notice of her fragile state.

The train stopped, and everyone rushed to disembark. Larry said his good-byes to Allen and bolted off the train. Diana collapsed back in her seat, while the other three remained behind with her. She was pale and shaking. When the train was finally empty, Diana spoke.

"The gravity of our situation certainly became apparent with all of those security forces today. I can't believe we all took this train, knowing what we know."

"We're either really brave or we're really stupid," Beverly said, also pale and shaking.

"Did anything happen with Haman?" Margie asked, "Oh, and Josh is really pissed off. He didn't appreciate hearing from me. The deal was to hear from you."

"I'll call him in a few minutes, he'll be fine. Anyway, Haman just sat with his phone off until we approached the Blue Bridge.

Then, he turned it on and started to type really fast, and the words 'POW RT successfully completed' appeared. I thought that was strange. I wish I knew what RT meant?"

"I don't think it really matters. What matters is that we're all safe and alive. I did learn a lesson from all this," Allen said.

"Yeah, what?" Beverly asked.

"If you see something, mind your own business," he said emphatically.

"You're probably right. Let's get off this train before we end up in the yards," Diana said.

"They all stood up, put on their coats and slowly trudged off the train and through the tunnel. As they neared the end of the tunnel, Diana caught sight of Tom standing in the terminal with his arms folded across his chest, lips tense, and a scowl on his face. There was no way they could avoid him. As the gang walked closer, Tom's arm came up, finger out: "You," he said to Diana, "come with me. The rest of you, get going. Now!"

"Tom, really, nothing happened, you were right, I need to get to work…," Diana stuttered.

"You need to come with me, now."

Diana obediently followed Tom to the room where he had taken the gang before.

"Sit," he ordered.

Diana sat, feeling very much like a child and not liking it at all.

"I thought I made myself perfectly clear last night that you were to leave the sleuthing to the professionals. What were you doing sitting next to Haman? Keep away from him! We took your concerns seriously, we added security on the train, and all of the trains so far are safe without incident. Butt out!" Tom shouted in a very intimidating tone.

"But…" Diana attempted to speak.

"No buts, no anything. If I catch you playing detective again, I will arrest you. I have just two words for you, Doc—Patriot Act. Get out of here. Now."

Diana stood up. She looked Tom in the eye and slowly said, "Tom, don't you ever threaten me again!" Then she turned and stormed out of the room, panting with fear.

She entered the Graybar Building for a morning of research and writing, which she knew would not be happening. She sat in her office, thinking and recapping all the events that led up to this morning's commute and Tom's harsh scolding. Something was very wrong, but she just couldn't figure out what it was. Not yet, anyway.

CHAPTER 39

THOSE LITTLE GREY CELLS WORKING OVERTIME

It was Saturday morning, and Diana sat at her kitchen table, sipping her first cup of coffee. Working full time, even though her jobs were spread over many and various endeavors, left little time for life's errands, so she had written down a list of places she had to visit today in an order that made gas-guzzling sense. She was still concerned about the train episode,—or lack of one—so she decided to add one more location to her errand list. She stood up and went into the family room to get the portable phone. She dialed Margie, who answered on the second ring.

"Margie, are you going to be around today?" she asked.

"Yes, for about an hour, then I have to get to the supermarket and a few other places on my list. Why?"

"Do you happen to have all of the notes you were recording on our Haman situation?"

"Yeah, I do. Has Haman become a 'situation'?" she asked teasingly.

"Well, what would you call it? A catastrophe? A calamity? A mishap? A disaster? A..."

"Okay, let's call it our little situation. When do you want to pick up the notes?" Margie asked.

"I can make you my first stop on my errand list, if that's all right with you?"

"Sure, don't you just hate Saturday errands? We should plan a fun Saturday, maybe a spa day or something," Margie suggested. "Just to avoid those lists."

"I couldn't agree with you more. We'll have to pick a date, but it'll have to wait until…"

"I know, life always gets in the way of fun. Schedules, commitments, all of that crap…Oops, sorry about that," Margie apologized.

Diana held the phone and just smiled. Margie was so prim and correct that when she slipped in a zinger, her guilt just became too overwhelming for her. "See you in a few minutes," she said and hung up the phone.

Diana stopped at Margie's house, grabbed her notes, made her apologies, and completed her appointed rounds. When she finally returned home around 2:30, she was famished, so she made herself a quick sandwich. Then she decided to grade the tests she had been avoiding for the last week. She was so intent on her task that she forgot the time. It was only when she heard the garage door open, indicating that her husband was returning from his meeting with a client, that she looked up from the blue books.

"I will deal with Margie's notes tomorrow," she thought as she crossed the blue books off her amended to-do list for the day.

* * *

Diana rarely veered from her Sunday routine. She treated herself to reading the Sunday newspapers (three in all) and watching a few of the Sunday-morning talk shows. Josh joined her in these activities and added pancakes to the mix.

So it was noon before she spread out Margie's notes on the dining-room table to study them, since Josh had taken over their home office for his work. She decided to make a list of all of the suspicious events/facts and to note any that had been resolved:

Event/Fact	Resolution
1. Haman's relationship with PHEW	Haman member of PHEW
2. Haman and the shish kebob vendor	PHEW had him killed
3. Text message	No clue what it actually means
4. Threatening email	Sent by Tom to scare us into stopping our investigation
5. PHEW	People Hating Elitist Wealth, used to be a passive organization, now under militant leadership
6. Threat of train attack	According to FBI, no immediate threat or danger of attack
7. Haman works for uncle in mail-order hardware business	Supposedly to pay rent but could be other reason

Diana sat back in her chair to think. She knew the text message was the key to everything, so she pulled it out and read it over and over again. "What's RT? And, 7:20, is it really the time of the train that leaves the Westport station?" She was about to give up when her little grey cells kicked into action. "Oh, wow, I think I've got it, by George I think I've got it!!!" she thought ebulliently and ran into the family room for the phone.

She dialed Beverly's number, but the phone just rang and rang. She was just about to hang up when an out-of-breath Beverly picked up.

"Oh, Beverly am I glad you're home! Listen to me, listen carefully and answer carefully, okay?"

"Okay, but let me take my coat off and sit down," Beverly said. "I just ran for the phone. We just got back from brunch. Hold on a minute."

Diana nervously tapped her foot on the floor and her finger on the phone, waiting for her friend to finally get comfortable. "She always needs to be comfortable," she thought impatiently.

"Now I'm ready to give you my undivided attention, shoot."

"When you were writing down Haman's text message and trying to read it off his phone screen, could 7:20 really be 1:20? Think! This could really be important."

"Let me visualize," Beverly said. She remained silent on the phone for what Diana thought was an eternity, but in reality was about one minute.

"Yes, that's very possible. My seven could, in fact, be a one. Remember, my pad was in my bag as I was writing, and I wasn't looking at what I was writing because I was looking at his phone. Yes, it very well could've been a one, not a seven. My finger could have slipped as I was writing and made it look like a seven. That's really a very…"

"Stop babbling and listen to me. I have Margie's notes, and I am attempting to figure this all out…" Diana began to explain.

"It's over," Beverly said.

"What do you mean 'it's over'?" Diana asked peevishly.

"Well, for one thing, after we were kidnapped by the FBI,

they were pretty emphatic that nothing was going to happen on the train, and Friday came and went without incident. So, it's over!" Beverly repeated.

"What about the POW message I saw? If I could just figure out what RT means, I know everything would fall into place."

"I'll make a deal with you. When you figure that out, I'll take your accusations seriously. Until, then, I am perfectly content with trusting the FBI and Homeland Security. Deal?"

"Deal. Don't you even want to know the significance of 1.20?" Diana asked, hoping to lure Beverly back to her side.

"No, I'm tired of being scared. I just want to continue commuting without thinking about trains blowing up."

"Fine, good bye," Diana said, hanging up the phone in a huff.

* * *

Diana needed to bounce her ideas off someone, so she decided to interrupt her husband. She hated to share these thoughts with him because he was an even worse worrier than she was and she didn't want to give him any more ammunition about her commuting on the train. But it was Sunday, and he was home and available. If what she was thinking was true, she needed to vent and vent now. She marched herself up to the office and sat down on a very comfortable brown-leather chair. Josh looked up from the computer. "Hi, glad you're taking a break," he said. "I could use one myself. What's up?"

"Take a look at this text message and hear me out. I think the seven is a one, and I don't think it's a train schedule. I think it's a date." Josh stood up, stretched, and retrieved the message from Diana. He then sat down opposite her and read the text message.

"Okay," he nodded, ready for the rest of her conclusions.

"I think RT is the key to what this all means. We know that the Friday train ride was uneventful, but the message I intercepted on Haman's phone implies that something went on. I just need to know what RT stands for. Any ideas?" she asked.

"Let's free-associate. Run train, rail train, rush train…"

"And Beverly would say renovate train. Let's get away from train lingo for a minute. Maybe the T is not for train."

"Well T in your world stands for test," Josh joked.

Diana let out a scream the entire neighborhood could hear. She ran over to her shocked husband and gave him a big hug. "You're brilliant, just brilliant! But now I have to warn everyone. How do I get a hold of Tom? What am I going to do?" She was ranting.

"Calm down, tell me what you're talking about."

"The message on Friday. I bet RT stands for RUN TEST, and the POW meant a fake explosion, and RT successfully completed means that the test run was a success. The date 1.20 is Monday's date, January 20. The train is going to blow up on Monday!" she announced to her stunned husband.

CHAPTER 40

A FRANTIC NIGHT OF SOUL SEARCHING

Diana sat with the phone in her hand contemplating who to call first. She was certain that the train was in real danger, but who would believe her? She decided to call Joe Venedri because she at least had his phone number. She dialed the One-Four, and someone answered the precinct phone immediately.

"I need to contact Joe Venedri. This is the crazy professor, Diana."

"We know who you are, everyone knows who you are," the gruff voice retorted. "And you can't talk to the Lieutenant."

"Can't is a strange word, of course I can," Diana replied in the most obnoxious tone she could muster.

"No, you can't," he quickly replied.

"Yes, I can!" Diana yelled.

"Lady, I don't have any patience for you tonight. The Lieutenant is away for the weekend and won't be back for a few days. I think he went somewhere in the Bahamas. It's his wedding anniversary and he surprised his wife. So you can't talk to him. *Capisce?*"

"Then I need to talk to anyone on the task force," Diana pressed.

There was a slight hesitation. "Don't know what you're talking about, lady," he finally replied.

"Don't toy with me. This is an emergency, and I need to talk to any task force member. They'll know why. Please," Diana begged.

"There is no task force," he said and hung up.

Diana sat back on her leather wingback chair, placing her feet over the side, and let the tears run down her cheeks. She had practically come to blows with Josh over taking the train on Monday and had promised him to seek help. She had no way of finding Tom and didn't know anyone at the FBI. They would probably deny everything anyway because Tom was undercover. Now what?

She dialed Beverly. "Hi, glad you're home. Listen, I did figure out the message, and I'm recommending that you stay home tomorrow. I truly believe the train will be attacked, and I don't know how to stop it." She tried to explain calmly as tears continued to stream down her face.

"Tell me exactly what you think," Beverly said.

Diana explained how she had deciphered the message and her difficulty in finding Joe. Beverly listened intently and finally said, "Diana, I believe you, but I also believe the FBI knows more about this than we're giving them credit. I have a big meeting tomorrow with a new client. I'm taking the train. Just tell Tom tomorrow. He'll know what to do."

"He threatened me," Diana wept into the phone.

"He what?!" she said with surprise.

"He said he had two words for me—Patriot Act," Diana explained.

"He was just trying to scare you again. You really are a relentless busybody," Beverly said with a giggle.

"This isn't funny. Josh wants me to stay home tomorrow, but

if something happened and I didn't try to stop it, I couldn't live with myself."

"You've always been a Goody Two-shoes," Beverly said.

"I'm going to call Allen and Margie. They also need to decide. Maybe they'll have another idea. See you tomorrow!" She hung up the phone.

CHAPTER 41
D-DAY

Diana stood on the platform in jeans and sneakers. She had decided to dress for action, just in case. Josh had reluctantly accepted the fact that his wife was a one-woman crime-fighting machine. That is, if she would again follow the fifteen-minute phone-call regimen.

As they'd promised, her cohorts stood with her on the platform. She turned and whispered to them, "If I see him, I'll sit next to him again. Margie, here's my phone. Do your calling thing with my husband. When you see Tom, tell him what I think is about to happen. Got it?"

They all nodded and Margie took Diana's cell phone. The train pulled into the station and they boarded. Diana glanced down the aisle and saw Haman enter through the other door. He took an aisle seat which was unusual for him. Diana approached and asked him to get up so she could sit in the middle. He rose without taking much notice.

The train pulled away from the station. Diana settled in and noticed that Haman pulled out his phone and again held it in his lap. He seemed a bit tense, and she thought his hands were shaking.

Tom was walking down the aisle and approached the gang.

Allen immediately got up and pulled him to the exit area to talk. Tom glanced down the aisle, noticing where Diana was seated; he listened intently to Allen and scowled at Diana. Finally, he turned toward Allen and spoke to him. Diana wanted desperately to know what Tom's reaction was to Allen's words, but she was afraid to move. Besides, to do so, she would have to disturb Haman and that would draw attention to herself so she just sat still. Tom and Allen stopped talking, and Allen returned to his seat. Tom continued down the aisle. When he stopped by Diana and Haman, he shrugged his shoulders, looked at the tickets and continued. Diana tried to glance down at Allen who also gave her a shrug. It seemed to mean, "I tried, but no cigar."

Once again, Diana was aware of each passing bridge. She felt her body tense, petrified that the next bridge would be the one to blow up, despairing that she had no plan to stop it.

Haman just sat still, clutching his phone. Diana realized that they were finally approaching the Blue Bridge. She thought, "Yes, this is it. Of course, it's going to happen here."

She noticed that he quickly started to type on his phone as they approached the bridge. She leaned over, "Give me that," she said and tried to grab the phone from his hands.

"Get away from me, you bitch!" he screamed, getting up and running down the aisle. Diana got up and rushed after him, screaming, "Stop! stop!"

Haman ran into the bathroom at the end of the train car and locked the door with Diana in pursuit. She started to bang on the door and scream, "Let me in! I really have to pee! Let me in, I can't hold it anymore!" As she kept banging on the door, her fists began to throb in excruciating pain, turning red and swelling. The passengers just stared at her; some just shook their heads in disbelief at her ludicrous behavior, but she continued to scream and bang, not knowing if this would be her last breath. In her frustration, she also started kicking at the door, yelling all the while that she needed to pee.

Allen, Margie, and Beverly had jumped to their feet as soon as they heard Diana's first scream and ran toward her. She turned toward them as they now approached and screamed, "Get everyone off this car! And get Tom, now! Hurry!!"

But Diana was relentless, oblivious to the action around her, banging without pause on the door and yelling over and over, "I have to go! I can't hold it in! I'm going to pee!"

Meanwhile, Allen and Beverly did as she told them and led the passengers into the surrounding cars while Margie went in search of Tom. The passengers, most of whom recognized each other from their daily commute, and aware that the gang were friends, obeyed direction from Allen and Beverly. Some grumbled, but the urgency of the situation overtook the moment as they filed out of the car.

Suddenly, a loud cry came from inside the bathroom. Haman sounded like he was in agonizing pain. "Someone help me, help me and get me out of here!" he screamed. Diana finally ceased her pounding on the door, realizing that the imminent threat was over. She leaned on the door, exhausted.

At that moment, Tom appeared with Margie.

"This had better be good," he said, glaring at Diana.

Haman was still screaming as Tom took out a special key to open the bathroom door.

"Step back, Doc," he ordered.

Diana joined Margie behind Tom. He opened the bathroom door and there was Haman with his hand in the toilet, contorted like a pretzel

"I can't get my hand out! Help, please help!" he begged.

"How'd you get your hand stuck?" Tom asked as he

approached him.

"That crazy lady kept screaming through the door, and I dropped my phone down the toilet. I went to get it. I'm in real trouble, I'm in real trouble!" he wailed.

"It's just a phone," Tom said. "It can be replaced." At which point, he glared at Diana.

"Have we crossed the Blue Bridge yet?" Haman wailed.

"Why?" Tom asked suspiciously.

"Have we crossed the Blue Bridge yet?!" Haman screamed in a panic.

The other conductor arrived. Tom told him to call ahead to the next station and have the fire department there to help free Haman's hand from the toilet. Then he turned back to Haman, who was obviously in distress.

"If you want to get out of this mess, you'd better tell me why the Blue Bridge is so important."

"No way, just get me outta here, now!" Haman demanded. "I got rights! Ow! It hoits! Get me outta here!"

"Does the Blue Bridge have anything to do with PHEW?" Tom asked assertively.

Haman looked stunned at hearing the word PHEW and let out a wail.

"What will happen ta me, what will happen ta me?" he repeated, moaning.

"First, you have to tell me what's going on and tell me now," Tom insisted.

"I think I know," Diana said. She leaned over toward Tom and whispered.

"Doc, I doubt it," Tom said, sounding angry.

"Oh, please," Margie interjected, quite annoyed. "At least listen to her. He's not going to talk."

"Okay, what's your current theory?" Tom asked reluctantly.

"I think his phone was going to detonate a bomb under the Blue Bridge," Diana said.

"How'd ja know!?" Haman yelled, looking bewildered. "Who's this bitch anyway?"

"Stop calling me a bitch or I'll put your other hand down the toilet!" Diana yelled back.

Tom walked out of the bathroom and pulled out his cell phone. He dialed it and walked out of hearing distance from them. He stayed on the phone for a couple of minutes and then returned to the bathroom. Haman's arm was now turning blue. He was obviously in agony.

"We should be at the station in a minute, just hang in there," he told him.

"He got his hand stuck because of the flapper valve," Diana explained. "Every time he pulls on it, the valve closes more tightly around his hand and cuts off the circulation. He could have some serious trouble here." She smirked.

"And you know this, how?" Margie asked in amazement as Tom's mouth just dropped open.

"Remember, I'm a jack of all trades. Josh taught me about it. I don't remember when, it's just a bit of trivia that I learned. Anyway, this is not going to be an easy task for the firemen. Be prepared to stay like this for quite a while," Diana said with a grin as she looked at Haman.

"Lady, shut up! Can't you get this bitch outta here?!" he yelled.

"This lady stays right here. What's your name anyway?" Tom

asked.

"I've rights, I say nothing!"

"Well, consider all of the rights you'll have in federal prison, you idiot," Tom said.

Just then the train pulled into the station, and the firemen entered the car with the biggest cutters Diana had ever seen. She really wanted to watch them in action, but Tom's cell phone was ringing and she was even more interested in that.

Tom answered the phone. She heard him say, "Yes, yes, good work. Send someone over here to get him. Thanks. " After he hung up, he motioned to Diana and Margie to follow him to the other side of the car.

"Please, take a seat," he told them. I want to make an announcement, but first I want to get Allen and Beverly. You all should hear this." They sat down as he left the car.

"Oh, Margie, when was the last time you called Josh?" Diana suddenly asked in a frenzy.

"Don't worry, we're on schedule," Margie said. "Call him yourself."

Diana took back her cell phone, hit redial and spoke: "Everything is fine. We've thwarted the attack, Haman will be arrested, and all's right with the world."

"And how do you know that?" Margie asked in disbelief.

"I don't, but I can't be bothered to call him every fifteen minutes. Let's face it, Haman can't hurt anyone as long as he's stuck in the toilet, and we've gone over the Blue Bridge without incident. So, we're okay."

"You can spin anything," Margie said.

After rubbing her hands for a few moments to ease the pain from her incessant banging, Diana's curiosity took over and she walked back down the aisle to the bathroom to see how the extrication of Haman's hand was going.

She peered inside to size up the situation. She noticed that the train bathroom was a very tiny area, perhaps four feet by five feet, consisting mostly of stainless steel. A stainless steel box ran the width of the bathroom and housed the toilet. It was designed like the toilets on airplanes, with no water in the bowl. The stainless-steel bowl took twists and turns, and there was very little room to maneuver Haman or his hand. Indeed, the hand was jammed so tightly that a fireman was disabling the entire toilet around him. Since the room was small and meant for one occupant, only one fireman could squeeze in to work on the problem. Thus far, he had removed the front of the stainless steel box but was unable to remove the pipe and release the flapper valve before it did any more damage to Haman's hand. The paramedics were waiting to take Haman to the hospital as soon as he was freed. But it appeared that after consulting with each other, the firemen had decided to cut around him and let the hospital personnel remove him from the pipe.

Diana stood by and listened quietly as the firemen and paramedics decided what to do. It appeared that normal protocol called for careful removal of the hand with the least amount of damage to the equipment because Haman was not in a life-threatening situation. But after removing as many of the components as possible, they couldn't see how to safely remove his hand. So they began to cut around the area in order to remove both Haman and the toilet.

"And we should really care that this smelly little train lavatory is damaged?" Diana thought in disbelief.

Just then, Tom made his announcement over the loudspeaker: "Ladies and gentlemen, attention. We are very sorry for the delay. We ask that you all disembark from this train. Another train will be here in five minutes on Track Three to take you into the city. We've had a medical emergency that is being handled right now.

Thank you for your patience."

"Yes," Diana thought. "Some crazy lady was banging on the bathroom door, screaming about her peeing problem, and the men with the straitjackets are on their way to take her to the padded room. How will I ever show my face on this train again?" She returned to sit next to Margie.

Tom entered their car with Allen and Beverly in tow. Allen and Beverly sat down. Tom stood.

"First, I'll apologize for not believing you," Tom began. "But I'll not apologize for trying to stop your amateur sleuthing." He paused. "It appears that the Doc was correct. That's all I can say for now. I have a team on their way here to take you down to headquarters for a debriefing. I'll meet you there as soon as possible. Talk to no one, other than FBI, got it?"

The gang sat there with huge grins on their faces and nodded. Diana tried to stand up, but as she did, her feet just collapsed under her and she fainted.

CHAPTER 42

EXTRA, EXTRA! READ ALL ABOUT IT!!

Diana sat in her family room, shoes off, her long legs resting on the hassock with the strongest drink she ever had—a glass of white wine.

Josh stood over her, aware of the stressful day she'd just endured but also knowing he had to give her the piece of paper he held in his hands.

"Read this," he said gently. "I printed it off of the Internet. It'll be all over the news tonight and in print tomorrow in newspapers worldwide. This story is big, and you're the heart and soul of it, like it or not."

Diana put down her drink, took the paper out of Josh's hand and breathed a huge sigh.

"You know how I hate this," she said and began to read it out loud.

"Today, local Westport resident Professor Diana Jeffries foiled a terrorist attack on the Metro-North commuter train. Showing unbelievable courage, she witnessed homegrown terrorist, Raymond

Cherry aka Haman, a member of the national organization PHEW, People Hating Elitist Wealth, attempt to detonate a bomb planted underneath the Blue Bridge 357 that spans the East River leading into Manhattan.

"Wow," Diana interjected, "the bridge actually has a number for a name—I didn't know that!" She continued: "Dr. Jeffries noticed something suspicious in Cherry's behavior 'I suppose after years of teaching criminology and working closely with the NYPD, you get a sense of something wrong. It was an impulse reaction, and if I was wrong, no foul, but if I was correct, which I was, lives were saved, including my own,' the professor stated." Diana looked up at Josh. "We worked on this cover story for hours down at the FBI headquarters, hoping the press would fall for this cock-and-bull story. It appears they did."

"Talk to me, hon, what went on down there?" Josh asked, sensing she needed a sounding board.

Diana put the paper down, picked up her wine glass, took a sip and sat comfortably back in her wingback chair.

"Tom made it quite clear that his cover was top priority, so a team of FBI agents came to fetch the four of us and basically ignored Tom, who seemed preoccupied with making calls on his cell phone, anyway. We were taken not to the main headquarters but rather to an ancillary office in Midtown. We were going there to be debriefed. We met with Tom's boss, and now I can appreciate why Tom hates him—what an S.O.B. He had nothing but contempt for us, and quite frankly, I don't get it. We saved his..."

"Okay, I get the picture. Move on," Josh nudged.

"Sorry. Anyway, he talked to us briefly, and then Tom showed up with another guy who looked vaguely familiar—where did I see him before? Oh, I know! He was one of the street vendors Tom met with the day I followed him. Now, I get it. All of those street vendors are undercover agents. Tom wasn't pigging out on junk food, he's not a street-food addict after all. Whatever."

She continued. "They told us that there had been a boat moored to the Blue Bridge Number 357 containing tons of explosives—you know, full of fertilizer and diesel oil. It had been designed so that Haman could detonate it from the train as we approached the bridge. Timing was everything. They believe that all the bomb-making ingredients had come from Haman's uncle's mail-order business. They were legitimate sales so his uncle wouldn't have suspected anything was wrong. They're searching the warehouse now for the sales receipts, etc. Since PHEW was under heavy surveillance, especially after that poor shish kebob vendor was murdered, they just rounded everyone up for interrogation and arrest. But here's the fun part," Diana said, smiling for the first time that day. "They're so paranoid that we'll reveal Tom's identity that Tom swore us in and gave us a low-level security clearance."

"He did *what?*"

"Well, he prefaced our debriefing with, 'We're not at liberty to divulge the details of this case to you,' and he used his most serious and intense tone of voice. His partner said, 'Tom, there is a way around this. After all, look at the role these four people played in foiling this terrorist plot.' Tom nodded. It was clearly rehearsed," Diana said. She started to giggle and it became uncontrollable. She finally was able to continue between laughs, "Tom then went to a bookshelf and pulled down a copy of the U.S. Constitution and had us place our hands on it and swear to uphold it. I thought you used a Bible for that? It was a hoot, but not at the time because we were still all in shock. Anyway, we were told that we were approved for the lowest level of security clearance, but we now had to swear to keep the terrorist-undercover task force, aka Tom, a secret. We swore, so now you're the first and only person I'll tell."

"Needless to say, I'm honored. But one thing is bothering me."

"What?" Diana asked.

"Did Haman understand that he was going to get blown up with the rest of you?"

"Good question. I asked Tom about that. It appears he's not the smartest guy. He assumed that his section of the train would make it over the bridge before it blew up and he would be fine. PHEW wanted to show that they were serious about their cause and willing to sacrifice one of their own. Poor Haman, he was clueless."

"Don't feel sorry for him, he almost got you and others killed," Josh said.

" I know." Suddenly she looked around. What's that noise outside?" she asked.

Josh walked into the dining room and peered out the window. "There's a group of people standing at the foot of our driveway," he observed. "I would venture a guess that we have a bunch of reporters trying to get a statement from you."

"That's not going to happen. I made my statement at the press conference today where I was well-rehearsed and surrounded by FBI agents who would stop me before I made an ass of myself. Make them go away, Josh! You've handled the press dozens of times. Please!" Diana implored.

"Diana, it's freezing out there, and sunset is minutes away. Trust me, they'll be gone before long or they'll all freeze to death before morning," Josh assured her.

"What about paparazzi?" she asked.

"Hon, I know what a private person you are, but let's face it. You're never out of the limelight. You've been the featured lecturer at prominent meetings and written up for all of the wonderful philanthropies you spearhead. Be realistic, you're a bundle of energy, and when you enter a room, everyone knows you're there. You can't hide from this, so just ride the wave. You can do it," Josh encouraged. "You've done it before."

"But this is different. I'm in unchartered territory—there is more I *can't* say than I can. And let's face it: The real story is not something anyone wants to get out. It would make the FBI, NYPD, and Homeland Security look entirely incompetent. They want to save face, having made me the center of the action, and keep on doing whatever they're doing to save the world."

"We have no plans to leave the house tonight, so let them all freeze! And as for the paparazzi, our windows all have coverings, and no one with any sort of fancy camera with telephoto lenses can pierce our window armor. Let me start dinner and you relax," Josh ordered.

"I'm surprised I haven't heard from Oprah yet," Diana teased.

"Oh, you have dear, you have."

CHAPTER 43

THE DUST SETTLED?

It had been a long night. Josh filtered all incoming phone calls, but it seemed as though the phone would never stop ringing. The reporters eventually did leave the front of their driveway without incident, but Diana was sure they would be parked out there first thing in the morning. She was right.

She and Josh pulled out of their garage to find a barrage of reporters blocking their only exit route. Josh hit the horn, knowing he was waking up many of his neighbors, but Diana was intent on making her usual train. The startled reporters jumped out of the way, photographers snapping as Josh sped down the street toward their destination. He was sure some of the reporters would follow them, but he had had the foresight to ask for a police presence at the train station to keep them away from Diana. She just wanted to return to her normal routine, or whatever that had morphed into.

Diana jumped out of the car and headed up the stairs to the platform before anyone noticed her. The police were everywhere, and most of the commuters assumed that their presence was a result of the bomb scare the day before. Diana took her place on the platform where the usual group of commuters was also congregating. It was painfully quiet. A few commuters nodded hello to her, but no one seemed to pay her any special attention.

Diana thought, "I saved their lives, and not one 'thank you.' What strange behavior."

Allen, Margie, and Beverly finally appeared. They were all in position when the train pulled into the station. The doors were way off this morning, so the gang had to fight their way onto the train, hoping they would get a seat. As they entered the train, they looked around. The entire car was filled with colorful helium balloons. The passengers were all standing and applauding, some whistling and yelling. Tom looked at Diana and winked. For once, the gang was entirely speechless. Tom finally quieted the passengers.

"Ladies and gentlemen, please, can I have your attention. Please take your seats. Diana, Margie, Beverly, and Allen, we are here to say thank you for your bravery and selflessness in rescuing all of us from what could have been a fatal terrorist attack on our train. We are here this morning to let you know that we are forever grateful. Diana, would you like to say something?" Tom asked, handing her a portable microphone.

Diana knew what his wink meant. All attention was diverted to her and the gang. Play down Tom; he was merely there to react to their heroism. In fact, Diana thought that was true, since he basically had ignored everything the gang told him. But she was prepared to play along, as instructed by the FBI the day before. "Don't blow his cover," they must have reminded all of them a dozen times.

"Thank you, Tom. Golly, I just don't know what to say. As I said yesterday, I just reacted to a situation. I really wasn't thinking about my actions, I just knew I had to stop Raymond Cherry. He was acting very strangely. I'm sure anyone of you would have reacted the same way if you were seated next to him."

The commuters were on their feet again, applauding and chanting in unison, "He-ro, he-ro, he-ro!"

Margie, Beverly, and Allen looked a bit stunned and speechless. They were glad that Diana had been made their spokesperson. The train started to pull out of the station, late this morning. The gang looked around for their usual seats, which today were outlined with bouquets of balloons. As they headed toward the seats, Tom took the microphone from Diana, "As a token of our appreciation, we have designated these seats as your official commuter seats. Therefore, a plaque will be placed on the wall here with your names, thanking you for your bravery!"

"Tom, that's really very nice, but a lifetime of monthly passes would have been a really nice gesture," Diana blurted out as everyone laughed.

"Well, I've been authorized to give you a complimentary monthly for next month. Sorry, that's the best I could do," Tom responded as the passengers all booed.

"We'll take what we can get," Allen called out.

The passengers settled down as the gang took their seats.

"What's with the 'golly'"? Beverly asked.

"I was trying to make it G-rated," Diana replied with a smile. You never know who snuck onboard this car. The press is everywhere. I have a reputation to preserve now."

"Golly-gee, I guess we're all celebs now. So we have to be more vigilant with our public persona," Margie agreed.

"You're always vigilant. You have to preserve SOAP's image. No one ever gave a hoot about what I said," Allen added.

"Well, you had better start practicing. Were your phones ringing off the hook last night?" Diana asked.

"I unplugged the phone," Beverly said. "No one was going to bother me."

"Well, we can all agree, this was our fifteen minutes of fame,"

Margie commented.

"Let's hope. Now, since we missed our Monday book exchange, what've you got for me to read?" Diana asked.

They all went into their bags and whipped out a book and started exchanging their commuter library.

* * *

When Tom came by to collect their tickets, Diana asked if he had time to grab a cup of coffee. He said he thought that would be a good idea, so when the train entered Grand Central, Diana said her goodbyes to the gang and waited for Tom.

They walked silently out of terminal onto Lexington Avenue. They walked in the howling wind toward Third Avenue where Tom led Diana into a Starbuck's. Diana sat down, and Tom went to get them coffee. He returned holding two cups and some delicious-looking Danish pastries.

"I didn't know how you took your coffee, so it's black," Tom said as he sat down.

"That's fine. It's hot and will warm me up. I'm always surprised how cold it is out there." Diana and Tom sipped their coffee in silence.

Finally, Diana broke the ice. "What's next?"

"What do'ya mean?" Tom asked.

"What's going to happen to Haman? Notice how I stuck to the script and called him by his real name?" Diana asked.

"Yeah, I'm impressed. We can't let on that you were on this guy's tail for the last two weeks. Haman will roll over now. He's just a flunky, so he'll sing like a canary."

"You're sounding like a Bogart movie," Diana joked, then asked seriously, "I suppose he'll have a trial?"

"Well, we can't disappear him. This was too public. You and the gang will have to be prepared to testify—but that won't happen for quite some time."

"Wait a minute, if we testify, the truth will come out about our suspicions and how we were…"

"I know, we haven't worked that part out yet," Tom admitted.

"I'm not lying under oath. It was one thing to deceive the public to protect your work, but I'm not going to continue with the charade in front of a jury. I'm serious, Tom. Really, you can't expect any of us…"

"Cool it. The truth, nothing but the truth. Besides, if Haman rolls over, we'll plead him out and there won't be a trial. Got it?"

"Thanks. I got it. So, the next time…"

"Listen, Doc, listen hard," Tom ordered. "There will be no next time,"

Diana sipped her coffee and smiled.

CHAPTER 44

QUACK, QUACK, QUACK
PUTTING ALL THE DUCKS IN A ROW

Diana hated loose ends, and she needed to tie them up. She had what she called her "Rules To Live By," and one of her most important rules was: 'Have all your ducks in a row.' She meant to accomplish that today. Allen was expecting her at his office at 3:00 p.m., but she first needed to stop at the One-Four.

She entered the police station, and this time the officer at the desk seemed to respond to her presence with a bit more deference. Not a lot, but Diana felt she was making some progress.

"Ah, Professor Know-It-All, now Heroine, you know where to go," he said with a half-smile.

Diana walked through the squad room. She noticed some staring eyes, but, generally, everyone seemed busy and oblivious to the fact that she was there. She approached Joe's office. His door was open, and she knocked on the door jam. Joe looked up from the papers he was leafing through and smiled.

"Well, our local hero. I'm glad you stopped by. Come on in,

close the door."

Diana entered, sat down, crossed her legs and took a deep breath, "Are we good?" she asked.

"Of course, why would you question that?" Joe asked.

"I know I'm a bit nosy and refuse to give up," she said. "I just didn't realize what we had stumbled onto, and it seemed to add stress to our relationship.

"Doc, I promise to continue helping you with your classes, and I would hope if you need me for anything, you'll be straight with me and seek me out," he assured her.

"Thanks!"

"I understand from Tom that you were quite the heroine yesterday. I just wish I could've been there watching you bang on that bathroom door. You certainly do think fast on your feet."

"I know. You never really know how you'll react to something until you're actually in the situation. It was pretty funny, but my knuckles will never be the same," she added. "Lucky I'm not a prizefighter."

"That's one profession I can safely guess you'll never pursue. You totally amaze me. But, seriously, how are you holding up?" Joe sounded genuinely concerned.

"I'm still in shock. The ramifications of what happened yesterday are just sinking in. I expect a big shopping spree in the near future to help me cope. Anyway, I won't keep you. I need to get to another appointment. I just wanted to know that you were still in my corner."

"Always, Doc, always."

Diana got up and walked out of the office. As she started to exit the squad room, some members of the terrorist task force entered.

"Doc, great job," one of them said.

"Thanks," Diana said with her head down. She was getting a bit tired of dealing with the adulation. She left the station quickly.

* * *

Diana stood in front of Allen's office. She inhaled and exhaled before she put her hand on the doorknob and entered. Allen was sitting behind his desk, engrossed in what he was reading on his computer screen. He looked up as she entered the room.

"Ready?" she asked.

"Yep, let's go," he said, standing up and walking toward her. They left his office and went down the hall in silence. Allen stopped in front of the office door.

"Is he expecting us?" Diana asked.

"Yes, he seemed pleased to hear from me. Maybe he read about us in the press so he's not so pissed," Allen said hopefully.

"You're probably right."

They paused in front of the door, then Allen hesitantly turned the knob and entered.

The receptionist looked up. "Have a seat, he'll be right with you," she said.

She picked up the phone and called to let him know they were waiting.

"You can go in now," she said.

Allen and Diana stood up and headed toward the office. They stood in front of the door and knocked.

"Come in."

They entered the room to find Mo standing behind his desk ready to shake their hands. Diana felt relieved already.

"I'm so glad you agreed to see us after our last meeting which was a bit of a fiasco," Diana said, "Now, here's a dollar. I'm retaining you as my attorney."

"What?" Mo asked, looking quite shocked. "Please sit down, I think we really need to talk."

Diana and Allen sat down. It was agreed that Diana would do the talking. The gang had not mentioned Mo to the FBI or to Joe, so this loose end needed to be silenced and silenced now.

"It's quite simple. Once I retain you, anything I tell you will be privileged and you can't tell anyone. Correct?" Diana asked.

"Yes, that's correct," Mo agreed.

"Then take the dollar and consider this your retainer fee," Diana coaxed.

"I'm a bit more expensive than that," Mo said with a smile.

"Trust me, this is quite enough. If you feel you deserve more, we'll negotiate," Diana said smiling.

Mo acquiesced. "I'm listening," he told her.

"Seriously, this conversation has to remain confidential," Diana stressed.

"So, I gathered. As I said, I'm listening."

"Here goes. As you no doubt read in the papers, our commuter gang stumbled upon a plot to blow up the train. But the public accounting of what actually happened has been whitewashed, as you probably deduced, since we were on Haman's trail way before the train episode.

"Yes, I was aware of that," Mo said.

"We were very vigilant about 'see something, say something' and notified our train conductor of our suspicions. We were ignored. I spoke with the police, but the FBI and Homeland Security were keeping them in the dark about PHEW, so we were acting alone in our investigation."

"What did your train conductor say?" Mo asked.

Diana was hoping she wouldn't have to go there, but she trusted Mo and, after all, he was now her attorney.

"He's an undercover FBI agent and told us to back off after he caught us following Haman," Diana said in a whisper.

"Ah, now I get it. That's why you retained me, to silence me because the FBI and Homeland Security dropped the ball. Right?"

"Life's a bitch, ain't it?" Diana said with a grin on her face.

Mo sat back in his chair. He knew he had met his match, but it was all for a good cause.

CHAPTER 45
THE GANG'S ALL HERE

Diana and Allen reached Jacques's just after Margie and Beverly arrived. They decided that they needed to chill out with an elegant Jacques dinner, indulge in some good wine and try not to discuss terrorists or crime.

After Diana and Allen sat down, as if by magic, two drinks appeared: a kir royale for Diana and a scotch for Allen.

"Wow, great service, how did…? Diana asked.

"We made sure," Beverly explained. "After all, you were a busy bee today, quacking away."

"Not exactly the correct analogy, a quacking bee. You tease me about my quack tendencies, but putting order into things gives you control and when you have control…"

"We know, life is good!" they all chorused.

"You actually listen to me, how nice," Diana said laughing.

"I assume ordering is out of the question," Allen said. He was such a pragmatist when it came to food.

"Absolutely! Jacques already told us he's in control," Margie assured them.

"Well, quack, quack, quack," Diana added.

"Funny lady," Beverly said.

"Well, I'd like to put things into perspective. Do you think we can move on with our lives?" Diana asked.

"No," Allen said.

"Really, why not?" Margie asked, sounding worried.

"This was a big deal, foiling a terrorist attack on Metro-North," Allen answered. "We saved hundreds of lives, thwarted a major terrorist attack in New York City, and showed how average citizens can be empowered." Clearly he had given this much thought.

"Wow, powerful stuff," Diana responded. "I'm impressed with us, but I don't want any more attention. It seems so unnecessary.

"I say, ride the wave," suggested Beverly. "It's bound to die down. With 24/7 news, other stories will pop up, replacing ours. Let's just go on with our lives, as normally as possible."

"A toast, to normalcy!" Diana called out as they all raised their glasses.

"To normalcy," they echoed.

* * *

It was dark and naturally cold when they finally left the restaurant. But since they had stuffed themselves with some of Jacques's best dishes, they decided to walk back to Grand Central.

"I don't want normalcy," Beverly blurted out as they walked.

"What are you talking about, Bev?" Diana asked.

"I loved having some adventure in our lives. I was getting bored with the status quo," she said.

"Then let's plan a vacation," Margie suggested.

"Great idea. I'm always ready for a trip," Allen agreed.

"Where would we go?" Diana asked.

"I guess we have to include our spouses?" Margie asked.

"I would assume so," Beverly responded sarcastically. "Ron wouldn't like to be left home while we go gallivanting around the globe."

"Ditto for Josh. But where would we go? I think this is a great idea," Diana stated, shivering from the cold and fantasizing about a hot Caribbean sun.

"Prague," Beverly said decisively.

"Why Prague?" Allen asked.

"I bet there is tons of intrigue in Prague. I want another adventure," Beverly said.

"Berlin," Margie suggested.

"Rome," Allen contributed.

"You just want to eat your way through Italy."

"Absolutely! Forget the spy game, I want some good pasta," he said.

"Are you all delusional?" Diana chided them, rolling her eyes in disbelief. "What do you expect is going to happen on our 'vacation'? I get that Beverly thinks she is now a super sleuth, but really guys, this is ridiculous!"

"She's right. I would like to find a nice place to retire," Margie said.

"Then we should go to Milan. They give all residents a free bicycle," Diana said.

"Really?" Beverly asked.

"So I've heard."

The gang entered the station and felt relieved by its familiar warmth. They quickly glanced at the departure screen to check on which track their 8:36 train to Westport would be arriving. Track 23 was the designated track, and they walked arm in arm and headed for it quickly, with only five minutes to spare before departure.

"What about Kiev?" Beverly pressed.

"Too dangerous," Margie said.

"Geneva," Allen suggested.

"Istanbul," Beverly offered.

"Now that has intrigue," Margie agreed.

"Stop encouraging her," Diana said.

"Paris," Allen said, continuing with his food theme.

"South Beach," Diana stated.

"Cuban intrigue, and we don't even have to leave our borders." Beverly was overjoyed.

As the four walked toward the train, Diana looked at her friends, and smiled, thinking that life was indeed not at all "routine." She was hoping to sway them toward a more sedate vacation—but she had the entire train ride home for that.

Suddenly, Diana let out a scream, fell forward onto Beverly, and they both hit the ground with a thud. Once again, they were tangled together in a heap of their fur. Margie and Allen started to laugh as Diana lifted her head and pulled Beverly into a seated position—just in time to see the back of a young man in jeans, a black down jacket, and red wool hat running away from them.

"No, no, not again, I can't do this again," Diana wailed as her three friends laughed until tears ran down their faces.

THE END

For Now!

ABOUT THE AUTHOR

Barbara Pearson-Rac

Barbara is a true baby boomer and product of the 60's. Her career consists of various and diverse endeavors including adjunct Criminology professor, coordinator of a national cancer research project, corporate IT executive, and the list goes on. She delves into each new challenge with a spirit of adventure since her expertise was always learned on the job. So, when she decided to author a novel, which to some would be a colossal task, to her, this was yet another part of her life long journey.

A New York City native, she spent her college years in Massachusetts and currently resides in Connecticut; lives with her husband and two dogs, and yes, commutes on Metro-North to Manhattan. She hopes you enjoy the book as much as she enjoyed writing it!

If you enjoyed reading "On Track", please let Barbara know at barbjpr@gmail.com

Coming soon – "All Ears" another Diana Jeffries mystery.

Made in the USA
Charleston, SC
16 August 2014